METEOR

DEFEAT
JUDGMENT DAY

J.D. MARTENS

EPIC Escape

An Imprint of EPIC Press
abdopublishing.com

Defeat Judgment Day
Meteor: Book #3

Written by J.D. Martens

Copyright © 2018 by Abdo Consulting Group, Inc.

Published by EPIC Press™
PO Box 398166
Minneapolis, MN 55439

Cover design by Candice Keimig
Images for cover art obtained from iStock
Edited by Amy Waeschle

LIBRARY OF CONGRESS CATALOGING-IN-PUBLICATION DATA
Names: Martens, J.D., author.
Title: Defeat judgment day/ by J.D. Martens
Description: Minneapolis, MN : EPIC Press, 2018 | Series: The Meteor; #3
Summary: Dustin and Karina struggle to survive in Europe, while Jeremy returns to Houston
    with renewed vigor to help stop the comet. Meanwhile, the United States Government tries
    to find out more about a terrorist organization, the Soldiers of God. While Suri recovers
    from a terrorist attack, Robert struggles to work without his "partner in science."
Identifiers: LCCN 2017946137 | ISBN 9781680768299 (lib. bdg.)
    | ISBN 9781680768572 (ebook)
Subjects: LCSH: Adventure stories—Fiction. | End of the world—Fiction.
    | Meteor showers—Fiction. | Teenagers—Fiction | Young adult fiction.
Classification: DDC [FIC]—dc23
LC record available at http://lccn.loc.gov/2017946137

Para Gabi, que sempre acreditou

1

READY, AIM, FIRE

December 20, 2016
An Undisclosed Location

Ian Hosmer sat on a hard chair in an interrogation room. *The trouble with being a Christian terrorist is that you go to hell if you kill yourself,* Ian thought.

That meant it would be a long, slow death for Ian. The room was dim, but he wouldn't have been able to see well anyway. His left eye remained only slightly open due to a woman punching him repeatedly in the face. He was handcuffed to the chair, and his feet were cuffed as well. There was blood on his hands and on his wrists. But any amount of torture was worth it. He had done his job.

"Who do you work for?" the woman asked

between blows. "You need to talk, Ian. We can do this all day," the woman said.

She had a nice voice. Ian hoped she was a Believer.

"God will judge all," Ian muttered.

"You worked for the fundamentalist terrorist group who call themselves S.O.G., or the Soldiers of God. Is that correct?"

God works in mysterious ways, he thought.

Ian pointed his beat-up head toward where her voice was coming from.

"We are not terrorists. We are agents of the Lord."

"Since when did the Lord allow murder?" a man's voice asked, surprising Ian.

There must be two people in here now, he thought. Someone clamped something on his toes painfully.

"Since the dawn of time people have died by His command," Ian answered. "God is coming. Jesus Christ is returning. Who are we to try to stop Him? Even now, we are taking control of the South, and other parts of the world. There is nothing you can do to stop Judgment."

"What other parts of the world?" the man asked in a frustrated tone. "Tell us what you know!"

Suddenly, Ian felt immense pain sear through him, starting from his feet, and he began to scream. Then, everything went dark.

• • •

Jeremy sat in Soldier's, the bar near the Johnson Space Center, writing in his journal, which was something he truly never thought he would do. He felt calmer somehow after these writing episodes, as if putting everything on paper gave him some clarity on the world. The bar was also an escape from living with his family again, which after living on his own in Colorado was almost more stressful than the comet. Writing things down helped calm his nerves and focus, so he began:

December 20th, 2016:
The past year has been pretty intense so far—a lot of

people are even calling it the worst one yet. In February I learned that a comet is on a collision course with Earth, and it's supposed to hit in around two years. One of the nuclear missiles meant to change its course fell back to Earth and destroyed Miami. It's hard to know what to say about that; maybe it's one of those things that's difficult to represent in words. That's how horrible it is.

These two astronomers, Dr. Robert Miller and Dr. Suri Lahdka, found the comet. Apparently it's uniquely dark, which is why it escaped detection for so long. We're lucky they found it, and since then they've been shooting nuclear rockets toward the comet to try to force it away from Earth's orbit. The first nukes will hit it in three months.

Since then, things have gotten a lot worse here. Many countries have fallen to anarchy, or had to rein in their borders to keep their nations stable. In much of the United States, extremist groups have taken over, especially in the west. Colorado and the Pacific Northwest have been taken over by a group who call themselves the Union Anarchists. Apparently they started a new society *without government, without bureaucracy. I was there—in Vail, Colorado—and sometimes I think about going back, but instead I'm going to try to help the United States stop the comet.*

In the more rural areas, a Christian fundamentalist terrorist group known as the Soldiers of God (S.O.G. for short) have taken over. I've even seen them in areas close to Houston. They have claimed responsibility for the Miami bombing.

Then, a week or so after I got back to Houston, a plane of scientists here in Houston got blown up just before it could take off. The S.O.G. claimed responsibility for that, too. Dr. Miller was not on the plane, but a girl I had just met, Dr. Lahdka, was. She was one of the few survivors of the terrorist attack.

I met Dr. Lahdka, Dr. Miller's co-worker, briefly. I called her a girl earlier, but she's a woman even though she looks so young. She must only be like twenty-seven or something, which is crazy. She is really smart, and started to teach me some programming as I looked over her shoulder at her project. She didn't tell me much about it, but it looked important. She just said it was some kind of side project, which I thought was weird because she should be focusing all her efforts on stopping that huge rock hurtling toward us. But anyways, I trust her.

I feel bad for her family after the attack, and I hope she gets better. Dr. Miller didn't tell me much. She's in rehab from major third-degree burns and a brain injury—I don't know any more than that. I never thought the military would be so important here in the United States, but now that I have this U.S. Government badge, I can see why people are pro-military. Oh yeah, I forgot, the military is everywhere! On the streets, in restaurants, absolutely everywhere.

Many people would say the world had already descended into chaos before the comet (which Dr. Miller named Shiva, after the Hindu god). The wars in the Middle East, Africa, the poverty and income inequality devastating most of the world's population, and the ever-growing threat of disease to the poor are all enough to make one wary of the state of our planet.

Fortunately, not everyone is bent on destroying the world. The United States has organized a multinational team of scientists and engineers dedicated to stopping the comet. There's Gerald Jan, the billionaire technology entrepreneur, who's building rockets to help the United States. I think he's building some kind of big ship, too.

One of the "good guys," Dr. Miller, has stationed me at the Johnson Space Center in Houston. The center is being run by someone suspected of being in the S.O.G., which is why Miller asked me to be here—to be a "trusting eye," he called it. It's been fun so far, kind of like being a spy in a James Bond movie, but I haven't been able to find out much. All in all, it seems like the Johnson Space Center has become less of a focal point for NASA. It might be because Miller and his team are gone, but I'm not sure.

Dustin and Karina must have reached Europe by now. I wonder how they are doing, and what they are doing. I hope they're okay; I have so many questions for them. It sucks that the government took over the Internet. My father always used to tell me stories about life without the Internet. I'd roll my eyes at him, thinking that the Internet would never go away! How wrong I was.

Other than the initial anarchy that Shiva brought, things have been getting back to normal—at least in Texas. It might be surprising, but even though there's the Union Anarchists, the S.O.G., and the government—who are all trying to gain power—life for civilians is pretty much the same. For a few days stores only bartered with each other, but since the military came back things are a lot more stable.

There's less good food in the supermarket, and the only way to communicate with civilians is by landline phone, but many people have accepted that they have to work against the comet—and by extension for the government—to save the world.

I keep thinking about Miami, though. It's gone, wiped out by that nuke. It seems like everything would have had to go wrong for that to happen—and apparently it did. They tried to warn people to leave, and tried everything they could think of to stop it, but still a lot of *people died . . . And the citizens of Miami couldn't do anything about it. That's the worst part—the fact that all of a sudden a bomb could fall on your head without any warning at all. It's scary and exhausting. I heard that most of Florida has since been evacuated, with many people having relocated to Georgia, Alabama, and Mississippi, because they're scared of being close to the launch point; they might get hit again.*

I probably would have left, too . . .

Jeremy looked up from his booth, through the smoke in the bar. Ever since the comet's discovery people started ignoring the indoor smoking laws. He hated it. Then Jeremy looked back down at his journal, turned a few pages, and started to write again.

Dear Anna,

I've been thinking about you a lot. I miss you. It's weird going to bed without you by my side. Your skin is always so soft . . . How are you? Are you happy in Vail? I am working a lot here in Houston, and I'm even learning some programming. It's safe here. I mean probably not as safe as Vail, but it's better than it used to be. And hey—at least there's no Facebook. I love not having it, and it feels like I have so much more free time than before, even though I'm probably busier.

Sometimes you forget how much someone means to you until they're gone, and then it's just—

"Ah, screw it," Jeremy mumbled aloud angrily.

He ripped the page out of his journal and crumpled it up, frustrated. It was the third letter he'd tried to write to her.

• • •

Robert looked nervously at his computer. His nails were nearly gone, he hadn't showered in seven days, and his gut churned. The island of St. Thomas was out of coffee—or so he was told—so he had been reduced to drinking the swill referred to as instant coffee. Whenever his mind wandered away from work, Suri popped into his head. He even prayed for her—and it was the second time in just six months that he'd prayed. Robert hated the terrorists for it, and then hated himself for turning to the same faith-based garbage. But there was nothing else at this point he could do to save her.

The bombs were moving toward Shiva, toward that great comet, eagerly racing to defeat and divert it, while Robert hoped his team's calculations were correct. Secretary Brighton sat next to him, quietly urging the IMPs to make it, and Dr. Ivanov and Dr. Campero sat in the room quietly. Secretary Brighton had organized the meeting to get more information on the nuclear rockets that had just been launched successfully, and were on their way toward the comet.

"According to our projections, everything is going as planned. We're preparing for next week's launches . . . " Robert began, before changing the subject. "So, about the guy you caught. The terrorist? Did you find out anything more about him? Or the organization he works for?"

"Robert," Brighton began, "I think it would be best if you focused on your work right now—"

Robert was not having it, and yelled, "Damn it, Brighton, one hundred and fifty scientists are dead and you can't even tell me what happened? I needed those scientists. They were crucial to saving the planet!"

Robert sighed and clasped his hands together before taking a long silence, at which point Dr. Ivanov continued going over the most recent launch specifications. When Dr. Ivanov was finished, and Secretary Brighton went to leave the conference room, Robert caught up to Secretary Brighton before he could open the door.

"Well?" he asked.

Secretary Brighton sighed, and then spoke. "Okay, Robert. The man's name is Ian Hosmer. He is a twenty-one-year-old unemployed college student. To our knowledge he is a part of the Christian terrorist group known as S.O.G., the Soldiers of God. He is a devout Christian from Waco, Texas, but never exhibited violent behavior according to his friends and family. We don't know anymore and are trying to learn more about S.O.G. through him. What we do know may seem obvious, but it's this: he wanted to kill the people who are trying to save the world, because he thinks the comet is a sign from God. A sign that Judgment Day is upon us, and the devout will go to Heaven, leaving the rest to go to Hell. He is basically your typical fundamentalist terrorist."

Robert wiped away an angry tear, swearing at Brighton.

"How the hell could you let this happen?" Robert accused.

Brighton got angry. "How could *I* let this happen? What about you? It was *your* programming that got hacked, wasn't it? Yes, we failed, and the plane bombing killed one hundred and fifty people, but the hack that killed Miami killed tens of thousands and turned South Florida into a nuclear wasteland!"

They were close to each other now, arguing like an umpire and a baseball coach over a third strike. The tension in the room was palpable, and Dr. Ivanov shifted uncomfortably in his seat.

"I'm the one working twenty-four hours a day to stop this comet from destroying the Earth. I'm the one who designed the IMPs and they will work—" Robert ranted against Brighton until Dr. Ivanov stood up, cutting him off.

"Robert, Mr. Secretary, zis bickering is pointless. Ve must move forward. Ve cannot expect to defeat ze comet while we also fight amongst each other."

Robert and Secretary Brighton stood next to each other, breathing heavily. They looked over at Dr. Ivanov and back at each other before taking a step back.

"He's right," Robert sighed. "I'm sorry. We must look forward."

"Agreed," Brighton returned, still scowling.

Secretary Brighton stayed in the conference room while Robert continued working. They were waiting for the updated feed from the LSST, the Chilean telescope they now had under their control. It gave them a near-live feed of Shiva's progress toward Earth.

Now, though, as they received data from the LSST, Robert translated the science-speak for Brighton and David Atkins, the PR representative for NASA. Mr. Atkins had just arrived from Houston. Mr. Atkins walked into the office and plopped down into a chair, tired but ready to work. The president wanted to give the people a reassuring update on the progress of Project Defeat Judgment Day.

Robert executed the model he'd been working on regarding the comet's speed, and converted the data he read into English that Mr. Atkins and Secretary Brighton would understand: "The comet's ices have begun to sublimate due to the Sun, meaning it's getting faster as it comes toward us. Luckily, these gases are working to our advantage, and are actually diverting the comet a little."

"Is this what you expected?" Mr. Atkins asked, scribbling everything on a small notepad.

"It's very good news, but no, we did not expect

this to happen for another month or so. For now, our main goal will be to adjust the IMPs so that they follow a slightly new trajectory. Obviously we must hit the comet enough so that it is moved out of a collision course with Earth, but it can only withstand so many hits before it splinters. This would be potentially devastating, since we would have to worry about multiple comets instead of one. Therefore we have to change our modeling, so I've put our teams of theoretical astronomers to consider the effects of this new development in terms of rotation, size, velocity, and other factors."

"You're sending more IMPs now, right?" Mr. Atkins asked, continuing to write.

"Well," Robert explained, "this is a little tricky. Since the Earth revolves and our two launch sites are fixed, we can only shoot from Earth when we can use the Earth's rotation to our advantage. We also have weather to take into account, but our next launch is a week from today."

"And where exactly are these launch sites again?" Mr. Atkins asked.

"One site is Cape Canaveral, and one is at a military base called the Vostochny Cosmodrome in eastern Russia. Vandenburg Air Force Base used to be active, but we've lost control of coastal California."

"I see."

"There's something else you should know, but I think it should be sort of 'off-the-record' since we haven't completely finished this project yet."

"What is it?"

"Well, the billionaire Gerald Jan has built a manned spacecraft capable of holding twenty nuclear projectiles. It will be ready to launch in roughly two months, and should be a tremendous help to us. Because it will be manned, and will have communication capabilities. It will allow us to have an actual visual confirmation of the explosions. Right now, when the IMPs come into contact with the comet, the first thing we're aiming for is a reduction in the comet's spin. The spinning makes it more difficult to control, which makes it more difficult to move away from Earth. So, we reduce the spin by hitting the comet with nuclear explosions close to its surface, which will heat it up and cause jets of sublimated gases to eject—" He cut himself off, then simplified, "Basically, it will cause parts of the solid comet to turn to gas. These gases will act like motors to slow its spin. Doing this will make each rocket's blast move the comet even more."

"That all sounds promising," Mr. Atkins said, looking pensive. "But these explosions are still months away from happening. Could you explain what you are doing now?"

"Yes, well, right now the comet is outside Saturn's orbit, but it's still very far away. Right now our biggest concern is making sure the IMPs that are traveling through the Asteroid Belt actually do."

"Could you elaborate on this?"

Robert looked to where Suri used to sit beside him to answer the question, but then remembered she was still in the hospital. He breathed deeply.

"Yes, as you know we've been sending IMPs to space consistently over the past six months, and when they cross the Asteroid Belt—which is in between Mars and Jupiter—we have to make sure they fly through all the rocks and make it safely out the other side. To do this, we are using several telescopes to map as much of the Asteroid Belt as possible. Then, we hand that information over to the theorists, who will make models that predict the best paths of flight for the IMPs. The teams programming the flights of the IMPs get this information, and make sure the flight paths are consistent with as much empty space as possible. The IMPs are meant to withstand small debris but we have to make sure they avert the bigger asteroids."

"Very well, is there anything else?"

Robert sighed. "In your press release, could you please thank all the people who quit their jobs and began working for NASA to help? It might make more people join. We need to build IMPs faster."

"I'm sure the American people—and those of

the world—agree that we need to fight to the last second," Mr. Atkins remarked.

"At least the ones working for us. There are those who do not want us to succeed," Robert replied, thinking about Suri and the terrorist attack.

Mr. Atkins flipped through his notebook before finally landing on a page and asking, "You said the comet was very dark. Do you mean it is made of Dark Matter?"

Robert rolled his eyes. "No! Please don't write that! Not dark matter, just dark as in 'not light.' I've already had to endure almost everyone calling it a meteor. Don't make me listen to people asking about dark matter now, too."

"Okay, sheesh. It was just a question."

"Sorry . . . it's a touchy subject amongst us astronomers."

"Apparently."

Mr. Atkins sat while Robert twiddled his thumbs, waiting for the next question.

"So," Mr. Atkins concluded, "we are still pretty

screwed. The comet is still speeding toward us, it's still projected to hit us. We are continuing to fire IMPs as fast as possible, and they'll most likely get through the Asteroid Belt. Even if we do hit the comet right now, we don't know enough about the comet's composition to know for sure if there are enough gaseous pockets to successfully move it."

"Pretty much," Robert answered.

The next photo from the LSST showed the comet, still in their crosshairs, hurtling through space just as before.

2

PUBLIC ADDRESS

January 4, 2017
Johnson Space Center, Houston

Jeremy walked into his new office at the Johnson Space Center, sitting down at the computer that Dr. Miller had provided for him. He had plenty of python coding he could learn. It was morning; Jeremy was supposed to have lunch with Janice.

Jeremy had met Janice Effran on the way to the Rockies; she was the daughter of a billionaire who was building a spaceship to escape the clutches of the comet's impact. Then, when Jeremy felt he'd needed to return to Houston to help in the fight against the comet, Janice followed, wanting to do the same.

Jeremy worked on programming some very

rudimentary modeling of the collision course of the comet with Earth. He figured if he was going to learn a new skill, it might as well be related to saving the world. Given that, it seemed the logical course to choose programming. He had been working on this for a few days, and was having some difficulty getting the numbers to fit the publicized orbital path that NASA provided.

By around twelve-thirty he began to feel restless and decided to walk around the JSC campus. It seemed like a lifetime ago that he was working for his father, excited to see scientists working and hoping it would look good on his resume.

As he walked around, he thought about Robert Miller and the task he had given him to look for suspicious activity, and particularly for a man named Matt Wilkinson. Mr. Wilkinson was an Evangelical preacher before the comet came, and had been involved in politics as well. When Dr. Miller heard that he had been put in charge of the Johnson Space

Center, he immediately called Jeremy to see if he could enlist him as a watchful eye—a spy.

So far, the man had kept to himself, locking himself in his office for most of the day. He arrived by eight a.m. every day, and left by five. On the few occasions he did leave his office, a personal bodyguard followed him everywhere—even *into* the bathroom.

"So that's pretty much it," Jeremy said on the phone to Dr. Miller now, relaying the most recent information he'd found about Mr. Wilkinson.

"Keep looking," Robert returned. "The man has access to a lot of important information. We need to know what he is up to."

"Right, sounds good."

"There is a team over at the JSC that I think you should join. Well, you don't have the PhD to join it per se, but I would like you to be my go-between. They are the Structural Integrities team. They are one of the most important teams working at the JSC. They're responsible for calculating the composition of the comet's upper hemisphere, which is of vital importance to choosing where to explode the IMPs. I am worried, or maybe just paranoid, that Wilkinson could try to sabotage Project DJD by doctoring the data they send me. We're only about six weeks away from when the impacts will begin.

"I get their data through a secure data-transfer method, so once it leaves their hands it goes directly to mine. However, I don't see the data automatically—they have to send it to me. So, if there is someone who wants to sabotage us, it would be someone on the Structural Integrities team. What I want you to do is go into their office, follow the instructions I emailed to you, and send me the raw data. Then, my team here will cross-correlate the data to see if any JSC Structural Integrities employees are trying to sabotage our work."

"Sure. How do I get into their office, though? You want me to break in at night or something?"

"Look in my right desk drawer. In it you'll see a black box with a combination lock. Type six-six-two-six. There's a blueprint of the building inside. The

Structural Integrities team's office is on floor three, room three-oh-four. But, many of them probably work in the cafeteria, since everyone has to collaborate together."

"Sounds good. And just out of curiosity, why six-six-two-six?" Jeremy asked, thinking it must be some kind of cool science number. He was right.

"They are the first numbers in Planck's constant. The smallest amount of energy there can be. Alright, I have to go. Thanks for everything, Jeremy. I'll speak with you soon."

"Bye, Dr. Miller."

Jeremy found the box, unlocked it with the code, and found the map. He also found a gun and some spare cash, which Jeremy thought rather odd considering Dr. Miller seemed like a simple scientist—not a CIA agent.

The Soldiers of God, the terrorist group responsible for blowing up the plane on the tarmac in Houston and for the botched missile launch in Miami, had initially lost a lot of support for their cause. Over the months, though, they'd still been active around Houston, and Jeremy often saw their propaganda on street signs and graffiti'd on the sides of buildings. *Despite their terrorism, they still have followers . . . unbelievable*, he thought.

By one o'clock, Jeremy stepped into a small diner down the street from the JSC. The diner was aptly named Spacefront, but inside it looked anything but futuristic. It was the quintessential American diner, complete with black-and-white tile floors, red booths, and swivel bar stools. There even stood a jukebox and a gumball machine nestled in the far corner of the diner. Jeremy saw Janice sitting by herself in a booth at the far end of the diner. She was rubbing her neck, stressed, but smiled when she saw Jeremy walk up to her booth.

"Hey, Janice, how's it going?" Jeremy asked as he slid into the booth across from her.

"Hi Jeremy! I'm doing great!" Janice replied.

Jeremy and Janice had been eating lunch together frequently since they both worked at the JSC. Before the comet, Janice had worked as a project manager for a Silicon Valley tech firm, so when she came to Houston she'd been given the job of overseeing a team of engineers at the JSC. She'd been working at the JSC since the day she arrived in Houston, a few days before the plane bombing.

A waitress came by and they each ordered cheeseburgers, and Janice added a milkshake. Janice was twenty-nine years old, and had blonde hair and hazel eyes. Her sharp features gave her a kind of countenance that obscured her subtler expressions.

"So," Jeremy asked, "any news of the Ark? Are you still talking to your dad or no?"

"He says they should be ready to launch in a year or so."

"I know he's your dad and all," Jeremy said, furrowing his brow, "but isn't it kind of messed up that he and the other billionaires are just leaving like this? I mean, just forsaking the Earth?"

Jeremy's water and Janice's milkshake arrived, and Janice sipped at her milkshake before answering.

"Don't get me wrong, I think the billionaires are cutthroat businessmen and they're definitely very self-ish. It's why I decided to leave the Ark. But some of the work they're doing is kind of interesting. Before I left, they were cataloguing as many seeds as they could, and bringing them aboard so they could re-cultivate Earth when they return."

"It may be interesting," Jeremy said, "but it sounds like they've given up and are just saving themselves. It's not hopeless. We can still stop the comet from coming."

"Maybe," Janice answered.

Suddenly, the TV in the corner turned on. It was an emergency broadcast, and President Chaplin stood calmly at the podium. Considering the tenuous political situation between the United States and many of the groups like the S.O.G., Jeremy was surprised that Chaplin made it onto the television in Texas at all.

"Good afternoon, my fellow Americans, and my fellow people around the world. This is President Chaplin, of the United States of America. I have come before you today to give you some terrific news. The deployment of Interplanetary Missiles that have been launched over the past month have been a resounding success. All twenty missiles are safely on their way, on a direct course to the meteor J312, and this is due to the tremendous international team led by Dr. Robert Miller. The Interplanetary Missiles previously making their way through the Asteroid Belt have all successfully done so, and for the next two months dozens more Interplanetary Missiles will be launched toward the meteor. I want to thank the international team of scientists led by Dr. Robert Miller for their hard work on this, and those of you who have joined our government work programs. Each and every one of you has contributed to saving the world. Thank you, and may God bless you.

"But we are not out of the woods yet. We need all the help we can get. And we need unity. To the people currently living in the rebelling areas of Washington State, Northern California, and Colorado, please know that you have an open invitation to join our noble cause. The United States of America has no interest in warring with states while all life on Planet Earth is under threat. I now urge the leaders of these factions of anarchy and religious fundamentalism to lay down their arms and fight against the true enemy: meteor J312. I would urge all of you who have lost hope, who have decided that there is no stopping this meteor, to remember that humanity's accomplishments are substantial, and we will persevere. Throughout humanity's history we have overcome adversity and enemies through hard work, a sense of justice, and above all, unity.

"For too long we have fought amongst our own species. For too long we have killed and massacred our own people, and left them dead in the streets. For too long we have let racial, religious, or class differences be barriers. For too long we have considered working individually to be beneficial universally. Let this impending threat unite all people, of all races, all countries, all religions, for the common goal of saving our planet. Each of us has unique gifts to share. Let us work side by side, thinking as one great mind, together, to conquer this enemy.

"Join the battle against the meteor."

Then, President Chaplin silently left the presidential podium, and David Atkins stepped up with details of how to join the fight for Earth. He gave them a website—actually the only website that the public would be able to use, since the rest was inaccessible. Mr. Atkins also told the viewers that any information leading to the arrest of members of the terrorist organization Soldiers of God should be given to the authorities immediately.

Their food came from an aging waitress who looked remarkably uninterested in President Chaplin's speech. By the end of the program, Jeremy looked over at Janice, who had finished her milkshake.

"The president kept calling it a meteor, but I thought you said it was a comet?" she asked.

"It is," Jeremy sighed.

• • •

Finally, we made it to Rotterdam! Dustin thought. Dustin felt like he'd made a huge mistake only three times on his journey with Karina to Europe. The first time was when he stepped onto the cargo ship in the Port of Houston, and seeing the Houston skyline for the last time. *I'm really leaving . . .* he had thought, and a terrifying dread swept over him.

The second time was on a particularly rough night on the Atlantic Ocean. They had been on the ship about a week. It was hard to remember exactly how many nights went by on that ship, since the days were always the same. The never-ending expanse of ocean surrounding them only facilitated feelings of endlessness, of lack of linear time, and of their own insignificance. Their gargantuan container ship was nothing compared to the vastness of the Atlantic. It was almost enough to make Dustin forget the comet had the capacity to restructure the very oceans on Earth itself.

Since neither of them had skills applicable to a large container ship, they were tasked with being the janitors. On that particularly stormy day, Dustin had to clean the engine room, a damp, dingy, dark nightmare. After the first two hours of cleaning spilled oil and grease, and repeatedly hitting his head on the low-hanging pipes, Dustin screamed obscenities until he was hoarse.

"God, what am I doing here? All this just to see some stupid monuments? Ahhhhh!"

The third time Dustin regretted his decision was when they landed in Rotterdam. He was overcome with a sense of dread. Rotterdam was Europe's largest port and went inland for twenty-five miles. So when the captain called Dustin and Karina to exit with their belongings—the same two backpacking backpacks they had in Colorado—Dustin looked at the vast port in horror. Almost all of it seemed non-operational! There were shipwrecked cargo ships beached on the side of the port. There was only one set of cranes and the rest were dilapidated hunks of iron.

Somehow Karina always managed to subvert his fears and calm him with just a quick grab of the hand and a smile. They began to walk south, down the N57. The trip on the ship had taken much longer than they'd anticipated. They made several stops along the way, going all the way up the East Coast before embarking across the Atlantic. Then on to Ireland and several stops in the United Kingdom, before finally making it to mainland Europe.

It would be a long walk all the way to Paris, and Dustin even joked that the world would probably end before they got to see the Eiffel Tower. Karina was not amused. They had spent Christmas and New Year's on that boat, and now the weather in Europe was frigid. They wore their biggest jackets as they started their hike.

They had been walking for several hours when a large semi truck drove by them, and Dustin stuck out his thumb, hoping that they could get extremely lucky on their first try.

They heard the truck downshift loudly, and it started to veer right onto the shoulder. Dustin smiled brightly at Karina as the truck driver flung on the hazard lights. They walked up to the passenger side of the truck, and Karina suddenly got nervous.

"Can't we just get into, like, a family's car? I feel like a semi-truck driver is the least trustworthy person on the road," she said, perturbed.

"Come on, let's try it, we didn't exactly come to Europe because we thought it would be safer here. Everything is screwed, and honestly I think we are super lucky—the first person we saw is giving us a ride! That's a good sign—and really, how many families are likely to just be driving around?"

Karina nodded, hesitantly agreeing, and looked up at the passenger-side window. There was a mild noise coming from inside the trucker's cabin, and the door swung open. Dustin looked back at Karina, shrugged and winked, and hopped in. Karina followed suit, climbing into the truck awkwardly with her large backpack still fastened tightly around her waist.

The trucker was slim, and despite the overcast weather, wore large sunglasses, a low-brimmed trucker hat, and thick denim overalls. The driver even wore a bandana over his face. The figure gave Dustin pause. *At least he's not a sweaty, greasy, energy drink–drinking hillbilly*, Dustin thought. The driver's hands were on the steering wheel, his thin, bony wrists visible between his long-sleeved shirt and his gloves. The driver's head slowly turned toward Dustin, seemingly awaiting a reply of some kind from his new passengers.

"Hey, um. Nice to meet you. We are going to Paris. Can you take us as far as you can?"

In response, the driver slowly turned his head back toward the road, turned the ignition key, and put the truck into gear. Dustin looked over at Karina, making a *well-that-was-easy* shrug, and off they went, south toward Paris.

3

THE PERILS OF FREEDOM

January 9, 2017
Charlotte Amalie, St. Thomas

Robert fumed at the screen showing President Chaplin's face and at Secretary Brighton in the conference room.

"Meteor? Meteor?! How could you still call it that after I told you a hundred times it is a comet!"

"Relax, Robert, is it really that important?" Secretary Brighton responded, exasperated.

"Yes! If it was a meteor then things would obviously be a lot—"

"Dr. Miller," President Chaplin interrupted, "I have a question for you."

Robert was suddenly aware of how loud he was speaking, and sheepishly replied, "Go ahead, sorry."

"What is my job?"

"President of the somewhat-less-than United States of America."

"Very funny. My job is to make sure you have what you need to make *comet* J312 not hit Earth. We have computer programmers that scoured what social media still exists on the deep web, telephonic conversations, and hidden microphones throughout the world, and determined that more people were talking about meteors than comets. To be honest, Dr. Miller, I do not care one bit if the population knows the truth about anything. I do not care if they like me, and I certainly don't care if they know the difference between a *comet* and a *meteor*.

"What I do care about is the safety and security of—not just the American people—but all life on Earth. If just one more person signs up to mine plutonium or flatten steel for one of your rockets because

43

the word *meteor* pricks up their ears, then I'll keep calling it a *meteor* until the day I die."

The room was silent.

"I understand, Madam President. I apologize," Robert conceded, still frustrated.

President Chaplin sighed. "We all have our positions, doctor. Remember that yours is to stop the comet, not care what the world calls it."

In truth, Robert knew this, but he hadn't felt like himself for a few weeks now. The comet had a psychological effect on Robert in addition to his increase in work and stress. It made him reevaluate his decisions. *What if it really did happen, and I couldn't save the world . . .* he thought. *I would have spent the last three years of my life being miserable for nothing.* Then, he would take another five minutes and his emotions would change, and he would get ready again to fight against this great enemy.

Even though he and his daughter still rarely spoke, the possibility of making up with her gave him an extra boost in motivation to save the world. Not that the world wasn't worth saving, but for some reason saving it for her meant so much more.

Everyone coped with the changes differently. David Atkins's new role was essentially as recruiter for the effort against the comet, making him the world's most important headhunter. Although demographics of the United States were now harder to keep track of than the rat population of New York City, the number of people signing up to help in the fight against the comet was astounding. David Atkins sent people to every inch of the country to try to solicit workers, promising food and other essentials in return for help building rockets. The country's supply-and-demand system had broken down, and everything was being rationed: meat, clothing, gasoline, and even water. Age restrictions on workers were lifted, as were hourly restrictions. People were coming in from all around the country to help save the world.

Within two weeks of President Chaplin's speech, hundreds of thousands of workers came from the rural areas to factories to help stop the comet. Some were sent to Detroit to convert the old car plants to build hulls of the IMPs, and others to Tonopah, Arizona to convert a nuclear power plant into a plutonium-enrichment facility. Programmers in Silicon Valley stopped working on app ideas, and Robert marveled at how well the talented Silicon Valley computer geeks had programmed the rocket's telemetry.

Other recruits were working for Mr. Atkins, trying to create new ways to hire workers. Unemployment was at an all-time low for the United States (excluding the states that seceded). It was beautiful to see a nation, normally so divided, all come together and unite against the comet.

It's funny that it took a huge rock from space threatening to kill all life on Earth to unite us, Robert thought, *but hey, it's working.* Of course, there were those who did not want to see the world saved. After the Ian Hosmer terrorist attack which left Suri close to death, calls were made to try to reach Suri's parents in India. Robert couldn't imagine their reaction to the news that Suri suffered third-degree burns over her entire body, had suffered brain damage, and would need extensive rehabilitation to recover. She may not even recover at all, which was devastating to Robert for many reasons. Given the Earth's current expiration date, he really hoped Suri could get better fast enough to help save the world.

Project Defeat Judgment Day needed her. But Robert missed Suri dearly. It had been a long time since Robert had worked with such a bright mind, and in some ways her youth allowed Suri to think of things in a way that Robert would never have been able to conceive.

Robert was trying to get Suri moved to St. Thomas, so that during the course of her recovery she could still be part of the team. He knew Suri; she would want to be included, even though she would probably need the time to recover. She wouldn't want to be stuck in some hospital, far away from her work. The doctors were refusing to move her; they said it was too risky considering her unstable condition. He would keep trying. In the meantime, recovery would be the only thing on Suri's mind.

Robert sighed, sipping at his drink, and watched the sunset over the lush hills behind the city of Charlotte Amalie.

• • •

Dustin woke up to Karina tugging on his arm. He scratched his eyes groggily and looked around, and noticed that the truck was stopped. The driver had shut off the truck and was looking at the twosome, with the same bandana and sunglasses obscuring his face. He was pointing out of the truck.

"Where are we?" Dustin asked.

But the mysterious truck driver only pointed.

"I guess we just have to get out," Dustin sighed, looking over at Karina.

They hopped out of the truck and grabbed their bags. The driver nodded one more time, and then Dustin closed the door of the truck. They watched the truck speed off down the interstate and then it became clear why the driver had stopped.

They were in front of a huge border fence, spanning the entire horizon.

"So, this must be the border with France?" Karina said, turning around and trying to get her bearings. They walked the few hundred yards to the fence and the gate. It was weird to see such a tall and ominous border. It was guarded by men with big guns—guns that Dustin recognized from Texas. Killing guns.

Once they got closer they could read the signs on the fence, which read:

FRANÇAIS SEULEMENT
FRANSKE STATSBORGERE KUN
FRENCH NATIONALS ONLY

"We won't be able to see the Eiffel Tower," Karina moaned.

"Yeah, well, maybe we can go to Italy, or Switzerland. Though crossing the Alps in the winter might not be the best idea," Dustin reasoned.

Thankfully, many of the shipmates they'd come to know on their Atlantic journey had fought in the army, and carried MREs, or "Meals Ready to Eat"—small, portable bags of food which contained an entire meal, were very rich in nutrients, and could last years. They were so rich that they even included two small chewable mints, which acted as partial laxatives, if digestion did not go as planned. Dustin had picked some of these up before leaving the ship, so they had food. Dustin also had a water purifier, a tent, and plenty of lighters and matches to start a fire.

"How far is it to the Swiss border?" Karina asked.

"About a hundred miles," Dustin guessed. His pack already felt heavy. He looked at Karina, whose teeth were chattering from the cold.

"It might be good to find a place to hide out, at least for the winter. It's only going to get colder and snowier . . . " Karina offered, as they began to walk east.

. . .

Social media hadn't worked for months, which Jeremy had been secretly ecstatic about. No more Internet popularity contests. Experiencing what life was like before the Internet, which Jeremy had only seen in movies and heard about from his parents, came as a relief. The drawback was that there was no way for him to know if Anna was okay. It had been only a month since he'd left her cabin, and he felt awful about how they had left things. It didn't seem like a breakup at the time, just a break—that's all he'd wanted. He wanted to help save the world, and she wanted to live out the rest of her days in happiness—at least Jeremy thought this was the case. He wished he could have done both, but he couldn't help Dr. Miller from Vail. He wanted to explain to Anna that he still loved her and wanted to be with her. He wanted to explain that he didn't leave to leave *her*; he just wanted to help save the world.

Jeremy thought about this as he sat at the table with his father and mother, who acted like life was going on normally. In fact, his dad was acting like he hadn't a care in the world; it was weird. Jeremy's dad didn't read the newspaper before work anymore, but instead listened to the government announcements about the comet, and seemed not to give it much thought. And Jeremy's mom was treating him like he was still a high-school junior. She would sometimes pack him a lunch before he went to work. She even called it his school lunch sometimes.

"So, Jeremy, I heard on the radio that they are thinking of reinstituting the NFL," his father said. "A sort of motivational tactic for the working class, maybe?"

Jeremy couldn't take it anymore, and walked over to the phone to call Anna at her cabin.

"Come on," Jeremy muttered, tapping his foot on the ground anxiously as the phone rang and rang.

Finally, the ringing stopped, but unfortunately it was the machine that picked it up instead. *Maybe she's off hiking with her parents*, he thought. Jeremy slowly put the phone back on its hook and went back to eating breakfast.

"Jeremy, I need to talk to you about something," his mom said.

"Okay," Jeremy replied reluctantly, knowing it was bad when his mother "needed" to talk to him.

"You have been coming home very late, and your father and I think it would be better for you to get home by midnight."

"You want me to have a curfew?" Jeremy said, startled.

"Yes, well. If you want to call it that."

Jeremy was shocked. A curfew, now? After he'd lived on his own for months at the cabin? "Why?"

"Well," Jeremy's mom began, "It just might be better that way, don't you think, Earl?"

Jeremy's dad looked surprised. He scowled, as if annoyed at being included in the conversation.

"Yeah, I agree, Sandra," he said, and returned to his breakfast.

Jeremy thought he could smell something on his father's breath, and leaned toward his father to sniff his moustache. His father shot him a nasty look.

"Jeez," Jeremy whispered under his breath, glaring at his dad, "isn't it a little early in the morning for that?"

His dad didn't answer, and then louder, Jeremy continued, "I gotta go to work. I'll see you guys for dinner. *Before* midnight."

When not at the Johnson Space Center or home, he went to Soldier's. He found it oddly calming to sit in the booth where he had confronted Dr. Miller, and write. He couldn't believe he had a curfew, but also didn't think his parents would enforce it. Hopefully, they just realized that their son was living at home again, and as such, figured he should abide by some rules. It wasn't the end of the world. *At least they didn't ask me where I go so late at night,* he thought. *They'd be upset if they knew it was a bar. At least, Mom would be.*

Throughout his days, he thought about Anna, about how to contact her. To tell her he was sorry, and make sure she was okay. Whenever he thought about calling her now, his heart skipped a beat and he didn't know what he'd say, so the thoughts never again morphed into action.

. . .

Ian Hosmer woke up again. He couldn't tell what was day and what was night, or what anything really *was*. He heard voices, some male and some female, and he felt pain, and he prayed to God. One thing about the S.O.G. was they didn't tell their operatives anything useful, but that hadn't stopped him from shouting locations of fake headquarter locations when the knives went in.

He thought many times that he had made a mistake—that he *was* a terrorist—but then he remembered God. The government had hurt him as much as they could, but they still couldn't get what they wanted, because Ian didn't have any information they could use. Maybe they just wanted to break him, and Ian thought that was coming soon, but he held onto the only thing he could: when he finally did die, he would go to Heaven, and God would thank him for his service. The police or the army or whoever was torturing him would torture him until he died; there was no reason to set him free, and Ian knew that. He was ready to die. It was a powerful thing, to believe in something so true and righteous you could die for it . . .

• • •

Dustin and Karina, teeth chattering and hugging tightly in their tent, were acquainting themselves with the subzero temperatures of winter in eastern France. It turned out the French government had shrunk its borders so they could manage their security more easily, which made Dustin and Karina's journey to Switzerland shorter. Now, they were camped somewhere in the Vosges Mountains.

"We'll freeze to death if we have to spend any more nights out here," Dustin chattered.

"I know," Karina replied.

The next day they walked along the train tracks, keeping an eye out for villages or buildings where they could take cover. They endured three more nights in the bitter cold, but they built a fire that kept them a little warmer than that first freezing night. Finally, on the fourth day, they found two abandoned train cars on the side of the tracks. Evidently they had been left behind after a collision. Dustin walked up to the first one carefully, shining his flashlight into it.

"Karina!" he shouted. "Come quick!"

Inside was a shipment of pounds of dried meat! Dustin couldn't believe their luck, and Karina thanked God for answering her prayers. The overturned railcar offered them some protection from the weather, and the woods around them provided them with plenty of fuel for a fire.

"What do you think, Karina? Should we try to stay here until it starts to get warmer?" Dustin asked, chewing on a piece of beef jerky.

"I don't think we have another choice," Karina said, agreeing.

4

THE UNITED NATIONS
. . . OF SCIENCE

April 15, 2017
Johnson Space Center

Jeremy had been working at the JSC for five months. He sat at Robert's old desk, alternating between twiddling his thumbs and programming on Robert's old computer. So far, he had been unable to report anything at all to Robert about Matt Wilkinson, the suspected S.O.G. member acting as political leader of the Johnson Space Center.

Martial law was still in effect, ration cards were in use, and food staples were handed out at grocery stores. Almost everything about life felt like they were at war, and Jeremy imagined this to be what it was like to live in a remote part of France during World

War II, untouched by the fighting, but forced to give everything to the front. In any case, his pay included a few extra ration cards which he used to buy food and other things his parents needed.

The exact area the comet would hit on Earth—if it did—was still unknown, and Jeremy suspected that it depended on how much Robert's team could do, and when the IMPs would hit. He hoped that the government would do what they could to give people more time to evacuate in the event of an impact, so Miami would not be repeated.

Jeremy had brought Suri's computer to his room, and had been given access to it. He had found something interesting in it, something that he looked at for a long time. It was an Internet drive folder, only accessible with an Internet connection. There were two folders that were password protected and accessible via the Internet. One was titled "Gerald Jan," and the other was entitled "Plan Z."

Originally it had made Jeremy laugh. It was odd how much of the new world, P.K.C. or

Post-Knowledge of Comet, reminded him of the old one. "Plan Z" was the same name he had used for a zombie-related English class project in his junior year of high school. It was those little unimportant memories that reminded Jeremy so intimately that the pre-comet world was so recent, and yet completely irrelevant.

Jeremy sat at the Enter Password screen for a while, thinking that it might be rude to open Suri's private folder. He figured that it pertained to the comet, meaning it was justified, but it still felt odd snooping.

Since he was on Suri's computer there was no limit on failed login attempts. Jeremy tried some common passwords he thought would fit with the astrophysicist Suri Lahdka. Unfortunately but predictably, they were all incorrect. After staring back at the screen again for a minute, he turned to his programming terminal, and began to write.

Time flies if you're learning. Four hours later, Jeremy got two successive phone calls. The first one was from Dr. Miller, asking him how things were going at the JSC.

"Okay," Jeremy replied. "So far I still haven't found out anything about you-know-who."

"That's alright. Just remember to notice any locked doors, hushed conversations, that kind of thing. We can't afford to have another terrorist attack."

"I understand, sir."

Jeremy worked for another four minutes before the phone rang again. Since Dr. Miller was the only person that called that phone, he began by saying, "Hey, Dr. Miller, what's up?"

"Jeremy? It's Anna . . . " the voice said, delicate but assertive.

Jeremy's heart jumped instead of giving him the words to respond. After a few seconds, he gathered his thoughts.

"Anna, hey! Um, how are you? How did you get this number?"

"I'm good. I just got back to Houston, and your parents gave it to me."

There was a long silence, and it seemed like both Jeremy and Anna were gearing up to speak. Anna got the courage first.

"I'm so sorry for acting the way I did, but I was mad that you wanted to leave! I know you wanted to help the world and I should have been okay with that. I should have gone with you!"

"I'm sorry too, Anna. I shouldn't have left like that. I wasn't thinking."

Jeremy felt like he could see Anna smiling on the other side of the phone. He was smiling too.

"Do you want to get coffee, maybe, and talk?" Anna asked.

"Sure, I'd love to get coffee with you."

Jeremy spent the rest of the day coding with a goofy smile on his face.

• • •

Robert sat at a huge conference table, which was where he sat pretty much all of the time now. He looked around the table and was impressed at the faces around him. Or, rather, he was impressed at the minds around him. Today was a hugely important day. Finally the first IMP had reached the comet, somewhere around Jupiter's orbit. The first target was a large gaseous pocket in the comet's second hemisphere, called the Lower Hemisphere. The Lower Hemisphere Structural Integrity Team had identified the best targets, and Robert had confirmed the modeling results himself. The first few dozen IMPs would detonate their nuclear devices just above the surface of the comet. They were an hour away from impact.

Each of the scientists at the table had the flags of their home country in front of them.

"We look like the United Nations," Robert said.

"Only more useful," Secretary Brighton replied, to which everyone laughed nervously.

"Things are looking good, and I'm proud of everyone in this room," Robert began, "but much more importantly, things are looking positive right now. Our first few observational satellites have been monitoring the comet for a few weeks, confirming our Lower Hemisphere structural data."

"And the Upper Hemisphere?" Dr. Campero asked.

"I'm still checking up on that," Robert replied, remembering his suspicions about sabotage from the JSC. "But we have a month before we begin Upper Hemisphere bombardment."

"T-minus ten seconds to impact," an engineer said in the conference room.

Of course, due to the communication delay from the comet, the IMP had already exploded twenty-nine minutes previously, but the information from the observation satellite orbiting the comet could only transfer the information at the speed of light.

"Five . . . four," the engineer said.

Robert held his breath as he watched the photos of the LSST on the screen, next to photos and structural data from the observational satellite.

"One . . . "

Robert watched as the next photo from the LSST

showed a white mass where the comet used to be—meaning that the IMP had successfully exploded. There was a chorus of cheers from around the room.

"But it's just all white," the secretary complained, "That doesn't mean the comet's just gone does it?"

"No," Robert said happily. "It means that the nuke set off successfully! And do you see the timing? It's the exact time and location we wanted. Our first bombardment looks to be a huge success, but we need to wait for the next stream of data to come from the satellite to see the details of the impact."

"Oh, okay," Secretary Brighton said. "This is going to take a long time, isn't it?"

"Yes, we'll need to dissect this data as it comes every twenty-nine minutes," Robert said.

Robert spent the next several hours watching the data come through from the first successful bombardment. Then, the second IMP came into contact with the comet and it went off exactly as planned too. Cheers resounded from the conference room. The first impacts from the IMPs had been a complete success, and the comet was on its way to being diverted in the way the team had modeled!

Over the next few days Robert recorded all the new information from the observational satellites in order to calculate just how far the first two nukes had altered the course of the comet. He could barely contain his sense of optimism, of hope. *We can do this!* While he input data into the navigation software of the nuclear IMPs just leaving the Asteroid Belt, he got a call on his cell phone.

"Hello?"

"Dad! Oh my God, how are you? It's so nice to hear your voice."

"Yours too, Jennifer," Robert replied, tearing up. "How is everything?"

"Everything is good here. Frank, as it turns out, is a very good hunter. And little Isabel takes after you a lot. She is quite the little scientist already, picking up little leaves and bugs and all sorts of stuff and comparing it to some of the biology books in the cabin. She is even logging her findings in a journal. She is sharper than your average eight year old."

"I'm so happy to hear you are safe, Jenny. I'm not sure if you get news, and I know everything hasn't gone exactly as planned in the past months, but everything is going as planned with the comet. Our initial bombardments were a huge success. Maybe we'll actually stop this comet from hitting Earth. Heck, maybe it'll even teach us that as humans we can unite and live together. Today, scientists from all around the world worked together to stop this ice cube, so maybe we aren't all that doomed after all."

"I hope so, Dad. Try your hardest, for Isabel. My little girl deserves a long life."

Robert teared up just when he thought he wouldn't, and told her he would try his absolute hardest. Without knowing it, Isabel had lit a fire under Robert's wings.

5

DR. MARLON BEETLESWORTH

May 22, 2017
Downtown Houston, Texas

Amonth after the initial successful bombardments, Jeremy sat at Soldier's, his new home away from home, and waited for Anna to arrive. Jeremy got to the bar a little early, ordered a soda water and lime, and went over to his favorite booth, luckily unoccupied, in the back of the dreary bar. While he waited for Anna, Jeremy took out his journal and began to write. He was in the middle of a sentence when he thought he heard someone approach.

"Jeremy!" Anna said timidly.

Jeremy looked up from his journal, even stopping mid-word, and looked up at Anna. She wore a blue blouse and jeans. *Wow, what was I thinking, leaving her* . . . he thought.

"You look beautiful," he said.

"Thanks. You too."

"Would you like a drink?"

Jeremy waved at the bartender, who nodded and took his time making Anna's soda water as she sat down across from Jeremy with a smile.

Jeremy told Anna about Dr. Miller and his team's successes in St. Thomas and about his job helping.

"That's amazing! Is there any way I could help?" Anna asked.

"Yes!" Jeremy replied, beaming. "I'm sure there's something we can find."

They were silent for a while.

"I missed you, Jer."

"I missed you too, Anna!"

"I'm sorry, for everything."

"I'm sorry, too."

It wasn't that easy. Maybe both of them thought it would be, and maybe they thought that forgiving each other was as simple as just saying sorry, but these things rarely are. Then Jeremy and Anna talked about their lives, and what had happened to them since they'd been apart. Jeremy complained that his parents had set up a curfew for him. Anna mentioned that she was going to live at her house alone, since her parents were still in Colorado. Jeremy guessed they would come home soon.

Then Jeremy held out his hands over the table and Anna took them. They smiled together and called each other stupid. *Things are going to be alright,* Jeremy thought. *At least I have Anna back at my side through this whole mess.*

The next day Jeremy heard from his parents that the government had released another positive update on the comet.

"Pretty amazing, huh?" Jeremy replied.

His parents looked at each other, then at him.

"What's going on?" Jeremy said.

"Your father and I think it's time you start your education at MIT," his mother said.

Jeremy's mouth hung open. Go to college? Were they nuts? "We're being ruled by Martial Law, the comet is still heading for Earth, and the world is in chaos and anarchy. How is going to college going to fix any of that?"

"Do you think that hanging around the JSC all day will?" his mother replied, hands on her hips.

Jeremy looked to his dad, but he only nodded vacantly.

"We're just asking you to plan for your future, that's all," his mother said. "Think about it, okay?"

Jeremy figured the easiest thing to do was to nod at his parents. *Things haven't changed around here,* he thought.

The next day Jeremy sat in his office at the JSC. The first thing Jeremy normally did at the JSC was to check to see if there were any missed calls from Dr. Miller. No calls. He started to practice his coding skills. Finally he had found something useful for coding. *Dustin would be proud of me learning coding,* Jeremy thought. *I wonder if he is okay over in the Old*

World. Hopefully he takes good care of Karina. That guy can be kind of crazy at times.

Jeremy was coding a program that would randomly assign letters to a text-area. It was his attempt to hack the folder Suri had locked. It would run through passwords starting with six letters, which was the minimum amount acceptable for Suri's. It would enter a password, and if the password failed, it would then go onto the next one. For example, once Jeremy opened his program, it would automatically type: "A A A A A," and if that failed, it would type "A A A A B," and then "A A A A C" and so on. Eventually one of those combinations would be her password. Luckily, the computer that Dr. Miller had left him was very fast, so once he finished writing the program, he would be able to open the folder relatively quickly.

After about an hour of programming, Mr. Wilkinson arrived at the JSC with his entourage, which meant that Jeremy would track him. By now he had a pretty good handle on his movements, but today he did something a little different. As usual, he went into his office and was there from around nine o'clock to eleven, with two bathroom visits. However, normally he would go to lunch from eleven to twelve, but today he didn't exit his room. Jeremy watched from down the hall, but Mr. Wilkinson was conspicuously absent from the group that walked to the cafeteria with his security cronies. But when Jeremy left to get some food of his own, he saw Mr. Wilkinson walking in the opposite direction toward a door.

Quickly, Jeremy ducked back behind a corner. Mr. Wilkinson looked left and right cautiously, then proceeded through the door. Jeremy walked over to it; it was the office of a Dr. Marlon Beetlesworth. *I don't know anyone by that name working here*, Jeremy thought. The dull, scuffed nameplate told Jeremy that the office was likely abandoned. Then Jeremy turned around and walked back toward the cafeteria. *I'll go check it after lunch,* he thought, *that way Wilkinson won't be there and I can have a look around.*

Jeremy ate his bread-and-cheese sandwich in peace, relaxing. He was wearing a faded T-shirt, and that was another thing that changed since the comet was discovered: department stores were almost empty. Nobody was buying new clothes; what was the point? Plenty of people weren't even going to work. And people were spending money on other things: food and shelter mostly. Jeremy made small talk with some of the other workers still at the JSC, then decided to investigate Dr. Beetlesworth's office.

He was dismayed to find it locked. However, this was an older wing of the JSC, and Jeremy figured this door was not immune to the "credit card trick." He quietly put his ear to the door and listened, in case Mr. Wilkinson was still inside. He could hear nothing on the other side. Then, he pulled out his ration card, and wedged it between the door and the frame, and wiggled the door handle while trying to catch the latch. After a few minutes of this, while Jeremy worried frantically that someone was coming down the hallway, the door creaked open.

The room smelled rank. Jeremy covered his nose from the smell, stepped inside, and quietly closed the door behind him. The air was thick and heavy. It felt like the room contained three times as many air particles as there should have been. Jeremy squinted, looking around. Decaying boxes were stacked to the ceiling, and when Jeremy switched on the light, moths scattered in all directions. The extra light did little to make the place more visible, the tall box-columns shielded much of the fluorescents. *This place must have been unused since way before the comet*, Jeremy thought.

"It's like the world's oldest closet," Jeremy muttered to himself.

He reached in his pocket to get his cellphone's flashlight, but then forgot he didn't carry a cell phone anymore. *Darn it*, he thought, *just when I was thinking life was better without the technology of today.*

He moved toward the end of the room, his hands out in front of him, stepping high in case there were more boxes on the ground. He felt something scurry across his foot, but pretended not to pay it any mind, instead just stepping higher. He got to the back wall and was surprised to find no boxes there. Jeremy looked for a ladder to see what was in all these boxes, but couldn't find one. *That's weird,* he thought. *What's Mr. Wilkinson doing in here?*

He was all the way in the back of the room now. To his right was another stack of boxes reaching toward the ceiling. They all looked like Leaning-Tower-of-Pisa box buildings—as if they would fall at any moment. He tried looking in one of the boxes at eye level, and they were filled with books. He looked at others, and then to his surprise one of the boxes he tried looking in wouldn't open. He tried hard to open the flap but realized it was glued tightly—and more importantly—the entire column of boxes moved slightly. Jeremy could rock the stack of boxes back and forth with one hand. He realized that the column was a unit, as if all the boxes were glued together.

"What the . . . "

Jeremy shifted the fake stack of boxes, looking for

what, he didn't know. Then, on the floor, he saw the outline of a square door. A trap door. At this point, Jeremy thought two things. First: *Cool! I'm in one of those scary movies . . . this is awesome!* And second, after noticing the heavy round metal handle set in to the ominous wooden door: *This is actually really scary.*

After staring at the hatch for a minute, Jeremy thought, *Well, I've come this far; I have to open it.* If Mr. Wilkinson was going here to communicate with the S.O.G. then he had to know. He opened up the trap door and saw a ladder leading down to darkness. Jeremy swallowed, and stepped down on the rungs. He wasn't religious, but he crossed his heart anyway. *Just in case You're up there*, Jeremy thought.

About four rungs down, Jeremy saw a thin cord dangling from the ceiling, and tugged on it. The area brightened from one incandescent light bulb. Jeremy watched the tungsten filament light up, and then continued down the ladder. *Creepy*, he thought. At the bottom, he looked around, the shape of the filament still burning in his retina.

He stood in what looked like a bomb shelter. *I wonder if this is a Cold War relic?* Jeremy thought. From working at the Johnson Space Center, Jeremy knew that it was built during 1963, when many Americans were terrified that an atomic bomb would be dropped on their heads. *Even though we were the ones and not the Russians that did it first*, Jeremy thought.

Jeremy looked up and surveyed the dim room. There was a car battery with jumper cables. A table. Some tools and a hose. Two chairs. Jeremy cringed when he saw a man sitting, head bowed, in one of those chairs.

He was very bloody. It was hard to see his face. He was handcuffed but his hands were in front of him. His head drooped so low his chin touched his chest. His feet were tied to the legs of the chair too.

Jeremy suddenly threw up, spewing his lunch on the floor, but that did not wake up the man. He was utterly emaciated. Jeremy looked over to the ladder and back to the man.

"Hello?" he whispered, but the man did not stir.

"Hello!" he said, louder this time.

But the man would not budge. Jeremy crept closer, and heard the man breathing. Jeremy then felt an overwhelming urge to help this man, as many people would, but few would act on. Jeremy decided to act.

He took one more look at the ladder leading to Dr. Beetlesworth's office and got to work. He picked up one of the sharp blades on the table and began cutting the rope tying the man to the chair. The prisoner did not wake up once while Jeremy cut the rope.

Jeremy then put his handcuffed hands over his neck, turned around, and grabbed the man's arms. He lifted him up, and the man hung from his arms behind him, like in a pack-strap carry. The man must have weighed only one hundred and ten pounds or so, because Jeremy could easily carry him. The ladder was more difficult, though, as he could only use one hand to climb, and it took a while to carry the man up the ladder.

Jeremy realized when he got to the door adjoining

the hallway of Dr. Marlon Beetlesworth's old office that there was no way he could drag this mess through the halls of the Johnson Space Center. Even if he managed to get through the halls unsuspected, he would have to go past the military and their guns, checking everyone's ID badges.

He thought about what he could do for fifteen minutes before he ran out of ideas. Then, he started on the idea he thought was least likely to get him shot.

As gently as he could, he set the man down in the room, and closing the office door behind him, he sprinted toward his office, hoping no one would see him running. Young adults running always arouse suspicion.

"Anna! Hey, I need a favor," Jeremy wheezed into the phone when he got into his office.

"Jeremy, sure! Are you okay?"

"I'm fine, listen. Go to my house, and go up to my room. Under the bed you'll find three kilograms of salt, two bottles of laundry detergent, and a gun. Bring it to the Johnson Space Center."

"Why?"

"We need bartering material, and I'll explain everything when you get here."

"Are you hurting someone?"

"No, no, I'm helping someone, I promise."

"Then I'll do it."

"Great! Did your parents take the van to Vail?"

"No, it's here."

Jeremy punched air with his fist. "Then bring it," he said, then rushed back toward the cafeteria, where he'd seen bread being unloaded from big burlap sacks earlier. Jeremy slipped to the loading bay outside the cafeteria.

"Bingo!" he said, finding the sacks folded and ready for pick-up the next day. He grabbed a sack and ran back to Dr. Marlon Beetlesworth's office, dropped it off, noticing the man still propped up against the wall. Then, he ran out to the parking lot to meet Anna.

He waited for around ten minutes outside the JSC complex. Since Jeremy had the pass to get into the JSC, Anna got into the back of the van and covered herself up with a blanket. Houston drivers often tint their windows, even with mom vans like Anna's, so Anna would stay hidden.

They drove through security without a hitch. The security guards all knew and liked Jeremy—he sometimes gave them his extra ration cards. They reached the parking lot and drove to the corner closest to Dr. Beetlesworth's office, and in this respect they had a stroke of luck. There were only two guards waiting outside the facility, Jeremy knew them well, and they would be the only ones they'd have to bribe.

"Hey, Jim, Al," Jeremy spoke, holding the salt and the laundry detergent.

"Jeremy, what's happening? How's saving the world coming along?"

"You know, some days it's a little messier than others. That's why I came to talk to you guys."

"What's up?" Al asked.

Al was a big man, and the salt would be for him. The laundry detergent was for Jim, who was skinny as a pole. They were an odd team, picked up by the military right before the call of the comet.

"Well, I have two bottles of laundry detergent and three kilograms of salt, and three ration cards for each of you."

Al and Jim looked at each other, their eyes brightening.

"What's the catch, Jeremy?" Al asked.

"I just need you two to go get some water at the fountain over there," Jeremy pointed to his right, around the corner.

"But there's no water foun—" Jim began, before Al cut him off.

"I don't know, I'm feeling a little thirsty," Al told Jim. "Maybe we should check it out."

Al grabbed Jim by the arm and led him back around the corner.

"That was easy," Anna whispered, once she got out of the van.

"Their government pay is terrible. I figured it would be easy to bribe them," Jeremy whispered back, and continued, "I'm going to run in and grab him. Open the back of the van, and get ready to drive."

"Wait, *him*?!" Anna said, confused.

But Jeremy was already on his way. He ran through the corridor, and walked back into Dr. Marlon Beetlesworth's office. He expected to see the man still slumped against the wall, but instead there was a trail of blood on the floor. Jeremy followed the gruesome trail to the opening of the trap door, where the prisoner lay unconscious. The prisoner must have crawled to the top of the ladder before passing out again. *Why would he want to go back into that dungeon?* Jeremy thought.

Jeremy picked up the big burlap bag, and moved the bloody prisoner into a fetal position. He was so light that Jeremy figured he could carry him on his back in the sack. He didn't know why he was doing this, only that the man did not deserve to be tortured. No one did.

He got the prisoner into the bag and heaved, groaning under the weight. Then he stepped deliberately and heavily toward the door, careful not to allow the prisoner in the bag to swing. There was a short walk ahead of him, when someone could see him, and this time he certainly would look suspicious in the public hallway. He was reminded of a Dutch Christmas story he'd heard once. Apparently, instead of giving little children coal for being bad, their Santa Claus would take them back to Spain in the present bag and teach them how to behave. Jeremy felt like the Dutch Santa, *Sinterklaas*.

Luckily he did not see anyone, and by the time he reached the door, he was relieved to see that the two security guards were still away. He heaved the body as gently as he could into the van. The man must have woken up somewhat, because the body shifted a bit, maybe trying to make himself comfortable in the spacious trunk.

"Jeremy, what is that?" Anna asked calmly, seeing the bag move.

"I don't know," Jeremy said. "But *he* needs our help."

Anna looked at him, her eyes wide with compassion and worry. "Okay," she said.

Jeremy could almost feel her strength, and it lifted his spirits. Maybe her time in Colorado had given her new energy, or maybe she just wanted adventure.

"We'd better go before we get found out," Jeremy said. They drove off to Anna's empty house, with Jeremy waving to the security guards on the way out.

6

ONE NEW PROBLEM AND ONE OLD ONE

May 23, 2017
Somewhere on the French-German Border

Dustin looked up, seeing something that many would consider the ticking time bomb of his generation—comet J312, streaking across the sky. It was only a small dot amidst the stars, but it gave Dustin a grim feeling as it made its way toward them. *I wonder how far it is*, Dustin thought, wishing he'd paid more attention in his high school astronomy class.

Dustin and Karina had camped out in the wrecked train car for the winter. With the weather warming up and the canned food running out, they had departed and were walking south. They'd been walking along the French-German border for a week, hoping to find a way into the country so that they could get to Paris, but were having trouble.

"Are you sure you're reading the map right?" Karina asked.

"I'm pretty sure. I mean, you see this river here? Well, it's in France. But the border fence should be way more south. Maybe they changed their borders given all the stuff that's been happening?"

"Maybe. I don't know, Dustin. I'm beginning to think that this was a terrible idea."

"What? This is awesome!" Dustin said. He looked around the beautiful countryside. They were on an adventure.

"Dustin, we just spent almost the entire winter inside an abandoned train eating canned food. Explain to me how this is awesome?"

Dustin was unable to convey the feelings of absolute freedom he had felt ever since leaving the United States, so he said nothing.

The two found a small clearing a few hours after

sunset. They sat together over a fire, the flames dancing beautifully between them, as they discussed their next course of action. Dustin suggested they forget Paris and head toward Rome and Vatican City. Karina wanted to see Michelangelo's Sistine Chapel.

"Don't you think it's strange that no one is here? Don't you think it's creepy we haven't seen any other people?" Karina asked as they ate.

"It's the countryside. Plus, we've seen people. Remember the smoke coming out of the chimneys in that village we walked along?"

"I feel like we're hiding or something."

"Remember Texas and Colorado?"

Karina remembered well getting held up at gunpoint at the gas station. "Yeah," she sighed. "What about the Vatican? Don't you think that's going to be really crowded?"

"Yeah," Dustin agreed, becoming unsure of what they would do. Dustin was still wary of meeting any people for fear that they would steal or kill them in the anarchy. They hadn't seen very many people aside from chimneys billowing smoke in distant villages and the occasional farmer. But they always kept their distance, and Dustin didn't think they'd been seen. It was sort of fun, surviving on their own in the woods. Karina, however, seemed to be done with the wilderness, and longed for a hot shower and perhaps food that didn't come from a can. Dustin decided that they'd have to risk it together, that they would make their way past the Alps, and eventually to Rome.

• • •

Just twelve months . . . Robert thought as he looked up at the comet from his newest temporary home on St. Thomas. In reality he had been looking at it every night since it appeared in the sky, and even though for a while the change in its size was negligible, he was now beginning to see it get just a little bigger.

He was on his way to the hospital to visit Suri. He had finally managed to get her transferred. She had woken from her coma, but she was weak and confused. Her brain had suffered damage from the explosion; she had forgotten how to speak English. At first she did not remember her work on the comet, and that she was a brilliant scientist. But she was progressing, if slowly. Robert had hope that she would recover fully, but only time would tell.

Each time Robert visited the Schneider Regional Medical Center, he spoke with Suri, telling her what was going on. He did it at first because he missed her, even though she was sometimes asleep, or unable to respond. It became a routine. It also helped Robert remember exactly where they were in defeating Shiva, and it helped him vent his frustrations. Suri was still deep in her recovery. Her burns were very painful, she required several skin graft surgeries, and she slept often, or cried without knowing why. So although she couldn't help Dr. Miller just yet, she listened.

Robert went into her room. She was asleep. He said hello to her, and she woke up, rubbing her eyes. She mumbled and closed her eyes again. Robert made sure her covers were tucked around her, and then settled into the chair next to the bed.

"So, we are on schedule," Robert told her. "The jets are effectively pushing Shiva farther away with every IMP we blast. We have a large percentage of the world working on our side, bringing us raw materials, building our IMPs, and firing them when we tell them to. It's been revolutionary, how well we've been working together and collaborating. It's also been really impressive how so many people joined in President Chaplin's Save the World work program. I'm sure in history classes in the future, they will look on her as a champion of the workers. Roosevelt's New Deal was nothing. It was good, don't get me wrong, but Chaplin is something else."

Suri mumbled, then yawned and blinked her eyes open.

"I just hope the blue collar workers feel the same way. There's no way we would be able to build bomb after bomb, engine after engine, rocket hull after rocket hull, if it wasn't for them manufacturing it all for us. I wish I could thank them somehow. The Upper Hemisphere Structural Integrities Team have said that the comet is still holding up."

"Are they still in Houston?" Suri asked foggily, as she sat up in her hospital bed.

"Oh!" Robert said, remembering something he'd asked Jeremy to do a long time ago but never got around to asking about. "I just remembered—I need to go check some data about their ammonia percentage . . . "

Robert trailed off in thought, then wrote some figures in his notebook. "Something weird did happen yesterday, though. A private jet arrived at the Charlotte Amalie Airport. Apparently, a man with government credentials stepped out of the plane, only to be quickly escorted back onto the plane and sent away."

When Robert looked back over at Suri, however, she had fallen back asleep.

Robert left the hospital and got into his car. It was a car he had always wanted—a Bentley Continental

GT. The way he'd come to it was a bit of a funny story. On the other side of the island there used to live an incredibly rich colonialist's family. Robert wasn't sure whether their fortune came from sugar or something else, but the family had benefited a lot from some colonial enterprise. When the locals found out about the comet, they felt freed from their social and economic slavery, and chased the rich colonialist's family off the island. Most of his possessions—including his home—were redistributed amongst the poor.

One day, as Robert walked from the hospital to the rental car, he saw a man driving his favorite car. The man recognized Robert as the physicist in charge of saving the world. When Robert complimented the man for owning such a beautiful car, the owner just stepped out of the car and offered it to him.

"It might give you luck," the man said.

Then the man told him the story of the wealthy colonialist, grabbed the keys to Robert's rented Buick, and drove away. Robert had stood, stunned by the encounter, before getting into his dream car.

• • •

Jeremy and Anna carried the man into the guest bedroom. He was so weak he couldn't speak, and thus couldn't argue. In fact, the man couldn't do much more than look around. He was beat up, but it looked like he still had all his faculties. After all, he was breathing and he had a pulse. Anna got the man a bottle of water, but he fell asleep before she could give it to him. Together, Jeremy and Anna stood at the foot of the bed, looking down at their prisoner.

"Who do you think he is?" Anna asked.

"I think he's being held and tortured by Mr. Wilkinson, the guy who Dr. Miller said was affiliated with the S.O.G. Maybe this guy worked for the government."

"It's possible," Anna mused.

Through the prisoner's tattered clothes, Jeremy could see he had a cross branded on his chest.

"We should wash him," Anna said.

But Jeremy looked repulsed.

"Do we have to? I mean we did just save him."

"Jeremy, he can't stay like this."

Jeremy knew Anna was right. So together they brought him to the master bathroom. They found some antibacterial soap, and took off the prisoner's clothes. The soap smelled like lavender—the kind Anna's dad used to use. They turned on the water and set the prisoner in the bath, but he did not regain consciousness. Slowly they washed the dried blood off of him. He had many bruises, two of which shut his eyes almost completely. Anna then grabbed some Neosporin and they ended up using most of the tube on him. The man began to weakly hold onto them as they put him in some of Anna's father's old clothes. They changed the comforter to the bed before putting him back on it.

"He looks pretty weird in your dad's clothes," Jeremy acknowledged.

Anna agreed. He was wearing a light green polo shirt and some corduroy pants. He looked like he was in the movie *Fight Club* because he was wearing semi-professional clothing but had bruises along his arms and face.

"I think we have to tie him down," Jeremy said.

"Are you crazy? He can barely move!" Anna replied, aghast.

"I don't like the idea of it either, but we don't know who this guy is. He could be a murderer or something. We need to make sure that—in the event that he's dangerous—he doesn't kill you in the middle of the night. I mean, living here with him wouldn't be safe unless we did that."

Despite initially hating the idea, Anna found the logic in it. They found some zip ties in her father's office, and a desk chair. Having seen movies where people escape while sitting on rolling desk chairs, Jeremy took off its wheels. They reclined the chair as much as possible, and sat the prisoner on it. They put gauze around his ankles, which were raw from the rope at the Johnson Space Center, and went over that with duct tape. Then they taped his ankles to the legs of the chair, and put zip ties over that. They did the same thing to his wrists.

Jeremy looked at a calendar hanging on the wall—around one year until the comet was scheduled to hit. He looked back at their new prisoner, who was still unresponsive. Anna got a piece of paper and wrote, *You're safe. I am around the house. —Alice*

"Why Alice?" Jeremy asked, after reading the note.

"I just don't want him to know my real name in case he does turn out to be a psycho."

"How about we give this guy a name? How about Marlon."

"Sure," Anna agreed, but asked, "But, why Marlon?"

"I found this guy below the abandoned office of a Dr. Marlon Beetlesworth."

"Marlon it is," Anna replied.

Jeremy and Anna agreed that the prisoner would sleep at Anna's while they figured out what to do with him. They made some food they thought would be easy to digest, thinking perhaps the smell of cooking would wake him up. Unfortunately, he did not wake up, so they sat eating brown rice and chicken breast alone.

"Why did you do it?" Anna asked eagerly, wanting to ask Jeremy the question the entire day.

"I don't know," Jeremy replied. "I really don't. I just saw him, so messed up, so defeated, and I thought it was the only thing I could do. It's not right for anyone to be treated like that."

"No one deserves to be tortured," Anna agreed. "I think you did the right thing, even if I wish you'd tell me a little sooner you were going to do something crazy!"

Jeremy laughed grimly. "Yeah, sorry about that one, just consider it an adventure!"

"I don't like that word . . . " Anna responded, but smiled.

Jeremy, satisfied with the job they did securing the prisoner, borrowed Anna's car to go home to grab some things to spend the night. He looked at his watch and realized it was already 11:45 p.m., and he would not get home in time for his curfew. He groaned, realizing that he would have to have *that* talk with his parents.

He tried going as fast as he could but the mom van couldn't do much past eighty on the freeway, and screeched into the driveway at 12:08 a.m. So close.

When he reached the door, he was surprised to find it locked. He turned his key, opening the door, and closed it behind him. His parents were waiting on the other side.

"Where were you?" his mom accused. "You were supposed to be home ten minutes ago. Why are you late?"

"Yes, son," his father hiccupped, holding a full whiskey glass in front of him. "This kind of behavior is unacceptable."

"I was only eight minutes late," Jeremy complained. "And plus, aren't these different times? I'm nineteen, almost twenty. In normal circumstances I would be in college anyway, and I wouldn't have a curfew then, right?"

They argued for another ten minutes about the dangers of going out at night and of robbers. Jeremy tried to tell them that he had lived in the wilderness, that he had been taking care of himself for a whole year, but it was no use. Jeremy thought that his parents were over-worrying, and his parents thought they should be in control while under their roof.

"If you're going to live here, you'll respect our rules," Earl slurred.

"And what about you, Dad?" Jeremy accused, the tears welling up. "All you do is drink. You might not get hurt because you don't go out at night but you're killing yourself!"

"How dare you talk to your father that way!" Jeremy's mom screamed.

They stood there, parents against son, son against parents.

"You're grounded," his mom said, after the silence.

"I'm leaving," Jeremy scoffed. "I was only coming here to get some stuff to stay at Anna's for the night, but now I guess I have more to get."

"Well," Earl said, "we're not going to pay for your college tuition, so you can kiss MIT goodbye."

Jeremy couldn't help but snort haughtily. "You're not living in reality, Dad."

"Well, at least I am beside your mother," Earl said.

Jeremy shook his head. He tried not to think as he packed up some clothes and a few keepsakes. Most of his survival gear was in his car, which was still at the Johnson Space Center. He grabbed everything he needed and walked out, past his parents with their disapproving stares, and drove off toward Anna's house, thinking that it would be the height of irony if he got robbed now and had to return home.

7

NOT EXACTLY THE ANSWER WE WERE LOOKING FOR

May 26, 2017
Houston

The next day Jeremy woke up feeling guilty for the argument with his parents. He decided unconsciously, like many young adults, to suppress the obvious feelings of parental hurt and go to work, pretending that nothing was wrong. He made himself some coffee—a luxury in these times—and checked on their new roommate, Marlon. He was still asleep. Jeremy sipped his coffee.

"You're really a sleeper," Jeremy murmured.

Anna came downstairs a while later, rubbing her eyes. Jeremy sat in the kitchen making breakfast—bread with some butter.

"What time is it?" she asked groggily.

"Almost eight. Good morning," Jeremy replied.

Jeremy walked over and poured Anna a cup of coffee, smiling at her.

"Good morning," Anna replied, smiling. *If it wasn't for the comet, and the tortured soul probably not named Marlon in the other room, this is what life should be like,* Anna thought.

Jeremy was already ready for work, but needed Anna to drive him, since his car was still at the JSC.

"So," Jeremy began, "call me the moment Marlon wakes up, because he might be dangerous."

"Jer, we really didn't think about this. What are we going to do with him? Let him go? We have to at least question him."

"We'll figure things out when he wakes up."

"And this man, Mr. Wilkinson?" Anna said, remembering their conversation the night before. "Could he possibly suspect you as being the one who took Marlon out of that basement? Because it could be a bad idea for you to go to work."

"I don't think I really have a choice. Not going would be just as suspicious."

It still made Anna nervous, and if Jeremy was being honest with himself, he was more than a little nervous about returning to work too. He did not want to become the next person sitting in that chair under the office.

Anna dropped Jeremy off outside the JSC gates, and then drove to the factory where she worked. Jeremy walked first to his car. He reached in it and grabbed the large hunting knife he kept in the glove compartment for emergencies. He'd grabbed it— along with its thigh holder—before leaving Anna's cabin. He also grabbed his only gun, and tucked it into the waistband of his pants. He then walked into his office cautiously. Thankfully, no one was waiting for him. He turned on his computer and became elated. The program he had built had successfully opened Suri's mysterious folder entitled "Plan Z."

Jeremy excitedly clicked it open, but found it all incredibly confusing. He saw thousands of lines of code, and a lot of numbers. Curiously Jeremy noticed that the information looked a lot like the files he had sent to Dr. Miller about the comet's composition.

He ran the code and there were a lot of things he didn't understand. He sent it to Dr. Miller, just in case it was important. He looked to the end of the file. There was a section of text with a lot of big words and complicated mathematics. He scanned to the end, to a paragraph titled, "Conclusion." He excitedly read through it, and as he did he felt his heart slowly sink deep into his stomach.

I believe in the event the ammonium pocket in the upper hemisphere of comet J312 exceeds our projected volume by 3000 liters, then we risk fragmentation under the bombardment strategy set to begin in a few months. Based on preliminary satellite data from the Observation Satellites DHI-48 and DHI-51, I believe the ammonium pocket is larger than anticipated, thus leading to a possible fracture. The Upper Hemisphere Structural Integrities Team based at the JSC, using the same initial data, has concluded that the ammonium pocket will not exceed the projected volume.

Attempts to find discrepancies or faults in my own (and in JSC's) method have been unsuccessful. This means that we have two different possible outcomes. If I am correct, the comet will split somewhere between the 140th and 145th nuclear explosion (somewhere in the week of July 20th, 2017). The file "model 1" predicts the course of Shiva's fragments.

Jeremy frantically picked up the phone and called Dr. Miller.

"Dr. Miller, come on, answer, ans—hey, Dr. Miller!"

"Jeremy, how are you?"

Jeremy thought about the prisoner in Anna's parent's bedroom. "Uh, crazy, but something even crazier might be about to happen: I just hacked into one of Suri's folders. It's from a side project she was working on. I just sent it to you. It has to do with the data I sent you about the Upper Hemisphere Team."

"I wasn't aware Suri was working on a side project," Dr. Miller answered.

"She thinks the comet is going to split, sir."

"Hm. Current data from the JSC doesn't support this theory. The comet should stay stable, at least until it escapes our orbital path."

"That's not what Suri discovered. She actually looked at the data from earlier satellite images, and not the newer ones, and predicts a fragmentation. I sent it to you as well."

"How did you get into the folder actually? I assume she had it encrypted?"

"Yeah. I . . . um . . . wrote a program to create a bunch of passwords."

"You wrote that yourself?"

"Yeah, I did."

"That's impressive, Jeremy. Okay, I have the file now. I'll look into this and see if it is credible. But you see the problem if it is, right?"

"It means that the JSC—and specifically the Upper

Hemisphere Structural Integrities Team—is lying to you."

"Exactly. This is not good. I'll get back to you on what is happening. Thanks for bringing this to my attention, Jeremy, you did good. It looks like Suri is helping us even from her hospital bed."

"Thanks, Dr. Miller," Jeremy said, beaming.

"Oh, and Jeremy?"

"Yes?"

"Be careful now. Someone may be watching you. If someone has been tampering with the data they could be looking at our communication somehow. I know it's supposed to be end-to-end encrypted, but who knows? We don't have the time or energy to make sure at this point. Just keep one eye open around you, and don't tell anyone what you found."

"I will, Dr. Miller. Talk to you soon."

• • •

Robert sat at his computer, a cup of coffee in between

him and his computer, madly typing and reading. He was trying to finish Suri's code as quickly as possible. *Why didn't I think to go over Suri's computer earlier?* he thought, chastising himself. Suddenly, Secretary Brighton walked into his office.

"How's my favorite scientist doing today?"

"Hey Nick," Robert said to Brighton distractedly. After eighteen months of working together, they were finally on a first-name basis. When the entire team was present, they still went by title, but alone they were comfortable enough to use first names. Not comfortable enough, however, for Robert to tell the Secretary what he may have found. Not, at least, until he was absolutely sure it was correct.

"I'm working on some figures for when I have to speak with David and President Chaplin on her next address," Robert said, knowing the Secretary would love to hear he was voluntarily working on public relations.

"Oh! Awesome, I'll leave you to it, then. I'm going

to be down at the cafeteria, if you finish early and want to grab a bite or a coffee."

"Alright, I might be down in a few."

Once the door shut, Robert got up and taped a hand-scribbled note on lined paper just above the door handle to his office that said, *Don't knock. Go away, unless it's INCREDIBLY important.*

It worked well. For the next three hours Robert fixed the bugs in Suri's code and finished it off, intent on seeing if the breakup was indeed possible a year before impact in Suri's timeframe. *That's six weeks from today*, Robert thought with dismay. If Suri's calculations were correct they would have to start on an alternative plan straight away. They would also have to scrap all the data they received from JSC for the last six months, which would put all of Robert's scientists and engineers on overtime.

Once he finished the code, he sipped the last of his coffee and packed his pipe. He had never smoked tobacco before, but after finding a pipe in his Bentley he figured cancer was probably the least of his worries.

He lit up, and clicked return, which started the model. It showed the comet being repeatedly blasted near its surface with the nuclear weapons as it rotated and moved through space. Below the schematic were dozens of figures detailing the composition and structural integrity of the comet, its distance to the Sun and Earth, its time to impact, and much more.

As the figures fluctuated and the comet's distance to Earth decreased, Robert watched in horror as Suri's model showed an eighty-five percent chance that the comet would fracture into three distinct comets, all with rocky nuclei. When it ended, Robert restarted the model and watched again as this time the likelihood became eighty-four percent.

Robert burst into Dr. Ivanov's office immediately, showing him the model.

"If Suri is right," he said, "we have two weeks before the comet splits in three."

"How could ve miss this? Who vas vorking on ze structural integrity of ze comet? Vas zat not your Johnson Space Station?" Dr. Ivanov accused.

"I think that there are some people over there who do not want us to succeed. What do you think? Is the model accurate?"

Robert paced back and forth while Dr. Ivanov skimmed over the math and programming that Suri had begun and Robert had finished.

"I am afraid you are correct," Dr. Ivanov mumbled. "I must call my superior officer to notify my country."

"Wait, no!" Robert said, putting his hand on Dr. Ivanov's shoulder. Dr. Ivanov looked coldly back at him.

"We can't let this get out now. We need to prepare. We have the ability to change the course of the IMPs, so we must do so, now. Someone is talking to someone else, doctor, and yes, you're probably right that it's someone in Houston, but they might be connected with the government. Whoever doesn't want this to happen is not powerless. We have to be careful."

Dr. Ivanov considered, and relaxed his expression, silently agreeing.

"If vee change ze course of ze IMPs without telling anyone, ze public might find out because vee are showing zem ze comet at all times. They vill think vee are trying to sabotage our own plan."

"It's a risk we're going to have to take. We aren't doing this for the medals, doctor. We are doing this to save the world."

"A medal vould be nice, though, don't you think, Robert?"

Robert laughed, "Yes, doctor, it would be."

"You can call me Ivan by ze way."

"Your name is . . . Ivan Ivanov?" Robert asked, momentarily forgetting the devastating news of the comet.

"My parents vere not very creative."

"That's funny, but alright, *Ivan*. Let's get to work."

• • •

Jeremy absent-mindedly practiced his Python programming while waiting for Dr. Miller to call him back. He spent a good deal of time staring at the phone, hoping that either Dr. Miller—or Anna—would call. *Mr. Wilkinson hasn't shown up yet, and it's already three o'clock*, Jeremy thought. *It must be because of Marlon.* Every time he heard someone walking outside his office, he feared they'd come in and arrest him. *What was I thinking?* he thought. *I shouldn't have involved myself.*

But he couldn't have just left that man sitting there. He looked as if his soul was almost out of his body, like only a part of it was hanging on, and the rest of it had already left for the next life. That image would haunt him for a long time to come. Finally, at around four-thirty in the afternoon, Anna called him and let him know that Marlon had woken up and was drinking some water. She sounded distraught.

"His name is Ian Hosmer. Do you know that name?"

"It sounds familiar . . . "

"He's the one who bombed the airplane!" Anna whispered frantically through the phone. "Get over here!"

Jesus, Jeremy thought.

After leaving a message for Dr. Miller with Anna's number, Jeremy rushed out to his car. He sped past the security checkpoint, almost hitting the boom barrier as it elevated to let his car pass through.

When he got there, he flung the car into park and jumped out of the car, running into Anna's house. She was waiting for him in the foyer.

"It's Ian Hosmer? That's the guy? What the hell?" Jeremy asked frantically.

"There definitely *was* a reason that the U.S. government was holding the guy! I don't know why I let you drag me into this," Anna decried.

Jeremy couldn't believe it. He had decided to commit a completely selfless act in saving a human being, but that human was a terrorist responsible for taking hundreds of lives. The sheer irony of the situation made him smile.

"Because you love me?" Jeremy answered.

Anna smacked him hard on the arm.

"Ow! Hey!"

"This isn't the time, Jeremy!"

"You're right, sorry."

"What are we going to do?" Anna asked.

"I don't know," Jeremy replied. "I'll think of something. I'm glad you're safe, though."

Jeremy kissed Anna and put down his bag. He felt his gun and knife on his person, thinking it smart to keep them there while they had a mass murderer in their house. Luckily, Ian was still tied to the chair. Leaving Anna in the living room, Jeremy walked into the guest room, where he found Ian Hosmer, formerly known as Marlon the Prisoner, the most notorious murderer and terrorist in the United States.

Jeremy was actually surprised at how young he looked; he must not have been older than twenty-four. He had a scraggly beard, short hair, no tattoos. He looked very docile in Anna's dad's clothes. He sat on his chair, squeezing a glass of water in between his thighs. Anna had stuck a bunch of straws together so that it reached his mouth, and he sat there, sipping from the glass of water in a polo shirt and corduroys.

"Hey, Ian," Jeremy said, looking calmly at the murderer.

"Where am I?" Ian asked groggily.

Jeremy ignored the question by asking one of his own: "Can you tell us what happened?" Jeremy felt dumb for asking, but figured that he had to start somewhere.

"Are you S.O.G.? You don't look it," the prisoner said.

"Um, no. I'm not. I'm for saving the world instead of destroying it."

"Saving the world? Look, I don't know about you but this world ain't worth saving no more. It's gone too far."

"So you blew up that plane to stop the scientists from diverting the comet's course?"

"I stopped those who are working side by side with the Devil to disrupt God's will."

"Right . . . " Jeremy had absolutely no idea what to do. Of all the people in the world, perhaps the most deserving of torture was the man sitting right in front of him. But, Jeremy could not return the man to that basement.

He also didn't really want him to stay at Anna's house. It wasn't safe. But he couldn't figure out what else to do with Ian. He couldn't very well bring him back to Mr. Wilkinson. Then Ian began to speak, not to Jeremy, but more in general. His face was still bruised and it looked like he couldn't use his left hand. It looked wrong, distorted. Jeremy looked at Ian as though he was a reflection in the water, like when you put a pen into a glass of water and it bends.

"The Day of Judgment is coming," Ian said. "Those rich billionaires thought they were just using some religious nut, but it was the religious prophet who was using them. I am the Second Coming, and so is the meteor. Those people of the Earth who have lived righteous lives will ascend to Heaven, and the rest will descend to Hell for all eternity."

Jeremy was about to correct Ian, telling him it was a comet and not a meteor, when a light switched on in his mind.

"What do you mean 'the rich billionaires'?" Jeremy asked.

Ian looked over at Jeremy. "You mean, you don't know?" he asked.

"I know about an ark being built somewhere in Colorado. The wealthy one percent will probably try to orbit around Earth—until the dust literally settles—and then descend back to Earth, avoiding the destruction that will occur."

Ian laughed then, before replying, "That's not the good part. They don't *just* want to save themselves. They believe that the world is ending, but not because of the meteor. They believe that global warming, overpopulation, and the general degradation of society is too much for our Earth to handle. They learned about the meteor when Russia did. One of the

Russian billionaires contacted some rich friends here and there, and they had a meeting. They decided that the meteor was actually a blessing in disguise; that the problems of the world were due simply to there being too many people on it. They decided not to tell anyone about the meteor and worked to build an ark.

"They would save themselves, and build a new world when they returned to Earth. A world not gorged with people. A world that is sustainable. Like Noah's Ark, the meteor is just the next Great Flood."

Jeremy sat, stunned by what he heard. He didn't want to believe it was true. The Ark, and those on it, accepted that they were allowing ninety-nine percent of the world to perish.

"But you don't think that—" Jeremy said.

"The world will end when the meteor comes. Those in the Ark will be struck down in some other way by the Lord. This isn't the story of Noah—it's the story of Revelations."

Jeremy still didn't understand the connection

between the billionaires and the Soldiers of God. Were they working together?

"What was Mr. Wilkinson torturing you for? Aren't you on the same side?"

Ian laughed again—a maniacal, demonic cackle.

"Mr. Wilkinson is a gutless preacher. He's no Soldier of God. He only wants to get onto the Ark. He wanted information that would help him win the favor of the billionaires so he could get on it."

"Did you give it to him?" Jeremy asked.

Ian laughed. "I had nothing to tell him. Judgment Day is upon us. Soon he'll suffer in Hell." Ian took a drink through his straw.

"So Wilkinson doesn't work for the S.O.G.?"

"Ha! Wilkinson's on his own crusade. He's been feeding false data to the scientists working on stopping the meteor."

Jeremy thought about this for a moment. He would have to find a way to tell Robert.

"What do the billionaires have to do with you, then?" Jeremy asked. This was still all so confusing.

"They wanted that plane destroyed," said Ian. "They saw the meteor as a golden opportunity."

"So," Jeremy said slowly, "Wilkinson told you about the plane?"

"Nope. It was someone else who gave me the information."

"Who?"

"I don't know. A woman who had a falling out with one of the billionaires. I think she lives around here. I can't remember her name."

Jeremy stood, feeling his heart sink into his stomach. *It was so obvious*, he thought.

"Was the woman's name Janice Effren by any chance?" he asked.

"That actually sounds familiar," Ian said, responding directly to Jeremy. "You don't know her, do you?"

But Jeremy didn't answer; he just felt the sinking feeling move further into his gut.

8

A BETRAYAL

June 14, 2017
St. Thomas, U.S. Virgin Islands

Robert returned to work without a break, though noticeably missing his partner in science, Suri. *She's helping me even from her hospital bed*, Robert thought.

Robert was now planning on detonating the IMPs directly on Shiva's surface. Previously, they had decided that a direct hit on the surface would be too risky, and make the comet unpredictable. So they exploded the bombs just above the surface maximizing the force to widen the chasm of the vapor jet. Now that the model showed that fragmentation would result in three comets, direct hits made more sense. It would allow them more control over their trajectory.

Robert quickly picked up his phone, calling Gerald Jan to tell him to speed up his launch schedule. He shared the fracture data with him.

"I understand," Gerald said, in typical form for him. "We have some work cut out for us, don't we?"

"How soon can you launch Vishnu?" Robert asked.

"I'm not sure. I'll give you a detailed response after I speak with my team."

Robert sent Gerald some of the data of Suri's model along with projections where all the fragments would go.

"It makes sense. I mean it wasn't like you could have kept on shooting the thing without having it break eventually. What I don't get is why you didn't figure it out sooner."

"Well," Robert said, slightly annoyed, "I'm afraid we may be dealing with sabotage. Without Suri's help

I'm afraid it would have been a lot worse. At least we have around a week now to prepare."

Gerald agreed, and hung up. Robert returned to work, fine-tuning the route changes of some of the IMPs, and he called in Secretary Brighton.

"What is it, Robert?" the Secretary asked.

"Well," Robert said, "there's a bit of a problem. Within one week, the comet is going to fragment into three separate comets."

Robert was silent as Secretary Brighton gasped. "What? Are you serious? What's this mean? How—"

"Calm down, Nick, it's not as bad as it seems. We found out pretty early, thanks to some modeling Suri started before her accident. For the past week I've been going over it again. By striking known weak points in the comet's composition, we can fracture it in a way that we can control."

"Fragments? You mean that we're going to be dealing with *multiple* comets now?"

"Nick, Nick. Listen to me. The good news is that

two of the fragments *won't* hit Earth a year from now. They will miss Earth in May 2018—"

"That's good!" Secretary Brighton said, interrupting.

"—and probably hit Earth around December."

"Dang," Secretary Brighton huffed.

"I know," Robert replied.

Secretary Brighton composed himself. "And the last fragment?"

Robert exhaled deeply before answering. "Unfortunately, it will still hit us on time. We are throwing whatever alternatives we've thought of, and I've directed all my teams to discuss alternative strategies, but I'm afraid we're simply out of options."

Secretary Brighton took a deep breath before speaking.

"Where will this first fragment hit? You said it'll hit in May?"

Robert nodded his head before Brighton continued. "How large is it?"

"It will be around seven kilometers in diameter upon impact, sir."

"And the others? You said they might actually hit us later, but how is that possible?"

"If our predictions about the split are correct, they will cross Earth's orbit twice during one Earth year. Once is in eleven months from now. Then, six months after that, they will again. The seven-kilometer fragment will hit in May, and then the other two will hit in December."

"What about the sizes of the other two fragments?"

"We project one to be twenty kilometers, and the other to be one kilometer."

"Okay," Secretary Brighton said. "So the medium one will hit first, then the biggest one, and a small one will hit six months after that?"

"Yes," Robert confirmed.

"Okay," Secretary Brighton said. "I'm going to speak to the president. I'll be in touch later today."

Robert had thought about telling Brighton the truth about the faulty information sent from the

Johnson Space Center, but decided against it. He figured it would be easier to simply work as hard as possible on changing the software for the IMPs and project the course of the comet and the exact fragmentation date.

To Robert, though this news was shocking; it wasn't so terrible. The comet would split, and only one fifth of it would land on Earth—which would destroy much of the vegetation and cause billions of deaths. But the planet would survive. Life would survive on Earth. *But we still have to worry about the twenty kilometer diameter comet*, Robert thought, pouring himself a drink before getting back to work.

• • •

"I always hated her," Anna said angrily. Jeremy had just told her that Janice was a mole for the billionaires building the Ark. They sat together in Anna's room, drinking coffee before work.

"What are you going to do about Janice?" she asked.

Jeremy thought for a moment. He was in a unique position because Janice didn't know he knew that she was a spy for the billionaires, but he didn't exactly know how he could use that to his advantage. He decided not to reach out until she did. He was also angry that she had betrayed his trust. *Could I have given her information somehow?* Jeremy thought, going through his conversations with Janice. *What information would she have found useful enough to give to . . .*

His heart sank. Jeremy felt a gut-wrenching dread and horror as he remembered telling Janice that the scientists were moving to the U.S. Virgin Islands. *I told her when the planes were leaving . . .*

Anna noticed Jeremy's sudden look of despair.

"What?" Anna asked. "Jeremy, are you okay?"

I can't believe it, Jeremy thought. The Sun set below the horizon and soon Jeremy would be able to see the comet streaking across the Houston sky majestically, and totally unaware of all the destruction on Earth it had already wrought.

9

MAJOR WINTER

June 22, 2017
Houston, Texas

"You know you're going to have to do something with me, right?!" Ian yelled into the kitchen, while Jeremy banged his head against the wall.

What do we do with this lunatic? Jeremy thought.

"You're literally only hurting yourself by doing that," Anna teased.

"Yeah," Jeremy said, "I know! But how do we deal with this? I tried to do the right thing by saving someone from being tortured, but it turns out to be the same person that may have ended the world with one stupid decision."

"It's okay, babe. We will figure it out together. It's

not getting better at work either though," Anna mentioned. "A lot of people are quitting."

Since she came back from Vail, Anna had been working in a computer chip factory. The chips were essential for the telemetry that allowed for the variable thrust capabilities of the IMPs.

"What do you mean?"

"Well, with the comet coming closer and closer, and the Soldiers of God threatening workers, I think people might have lost faith. Also, the government normally gives us a morning report on the comet and the progress in diverting it, but we haven't had the reports for a while. A girl named Sandra said she was quitting to live with her boyfriend in peace before the comet hit. I don't know, it seems like people are giving up."

Jeremy had noticed it too; there was an air at the Johnson Space Center that smelled like despair. Suddenly, he got a call from Dr. Miller on his government-issued cell phone.

"Hi, Dr. Miller, what's up?"

"You called me a few hours ago, Jeremy. What can I do for you? I'm very busy."

Suddenly Anna piped up. "Ask him about Ian, maybe he has an idea," she whispered.

"Actually, Dr. Miller, I do have kind of a predicament."

"Yes?"

"Remember that assignment you gave me? Well, I followed Mr. Wilkinson, and I ended up finding a man he was torturing. The man . . . he was so disfigured and I couldn't just leave him in that basement . . ."

Dr. Miller said nothing so Jeremy continued.

"I sort of . . . kidnapped the guy, and took him to my house. It was only later that I found out it was Ian Hosmer, the terrorist in the Houston airplane bombing."

"You have Ian Hosmer in your custody now?" Dr. Miller asked, shocked.

"Yeah," Jeremy replied slowly, "in my *custody*."

Jeremy thought about Ian duct-taped to the desk chair without the wheels in the house.

"I can't really give him back to be tortured."

"No," Dr. Miller agreed, "you can't give him back."

"And I found out some pretty awful news from him," Jeremy continued.

"Oh?" Dr. Miller replied, sounding wary.

"Mr. Wilkinson has been feeding the team in charge of the comet's Upper Hemisphere Structural Integrity false data. He's the reason the team didn't know the comet would split. It's not the team lying to you, it's Mr. Wilkinson!"

"I see," Robert said finally. "Let me think about what to do with Ian and I'll get back to you."

"Sounds good. Thanks, Dr. Miller."

• • •

Dustin and Karina continued walking. Karina was beginning to find their entire experience a bit tiring, and had slowly and discreetly been filling Dustin's backpack with essentials from her own to lessen her load. Dustin felt this every time, but it didn't bother him. Dustin happily walked on, listening to the chirping birds and the empty road. They were still in France, walking slowly south, the Rhine River to their left and the Vosges Mountains to their right. Beyond the Rhine was the Black Forest, shrouded in mist and mystery in the morning.

They were somewhere just north of the city of Cormar, in eastern France, when some train tracks came into view. Dustin noticed that the grass had not started growing over the tracks, meaning that this train probably kept running. They decided to wait on the tracks, thinking that one might go their way. Jeremy pulled out the deck of cards he had brought "just in case."

"You're not rolling your eyes now, are you?" he asked Karina. "How about some gin?"

She agreed, and they sat down to play. One

hundred fake dollars later, Karina reveled in her victory. Then, they heard a train rumbling north of them.

"You hear that?" Karina asked.

"Yeah, we should get on it!"

Within minutes, a large freight train came into view. It looked like those trains that homeless people live on; a train where getting stabbed has a high probability. Dustin had the idea that they would throw their backpacks in one of the open carriages, and then run, trying to catch up and jump in. There wasn't really another option, but Dustin was a fast runner and Karina ran track in high school, so they figured their chances were good.

They started off jogging alongside the tracks as the train rumbled noisily by them. The deafening mechanics of the train drowned out Dustin's voice as he yelled something inaudible to Karina. Karina was ahead of Dustin and she hurled her backpack into the train car. Dustin chucked his as well, and now they ran two train cars behind the one with their baggage.

They pumped their arms and legs and gasped for breath. Dustin thought about nothing else besides the open train car in front of him and finally jumped on, landing in a seemingly empty car.

They'd landed two train cars behind their chosen car, breathing heavily and hanging on for life. Now that the twosome stood in the train car, they realized the train moved rather slowly.

Dustin looked around and saw what looked like homeless people sitting in the car, eyeing them. Dustin eyed Karina, who looked scared. They walked along the edge of the train car, shuffling carefully along the outside edge to the mechanism hitching the two cars together and then jumped to the next car. They did this two more times until they finally found the train car where their bags were.

It looked like two families were in the train, each eying the newcomers suspiciously. It seemed that they did not particularly appreciate two strange bags being flung into their lives, followed by strangers coming into their train car.

"Hi, sorry," Karina said, awkwardly trying to reduce the tension. "Wait, hey!" Karina looked over and saw that a family of four to the right were rummaging through her bag. Luckily, a lot of the stuff she had was now in Dustin's bag, which was still lying untouched on the ground. The two kids from the family were hungrily eating the food out of her bag, but Karina wouldn't stop them; they were kids. What was she supposed to do?

"Let them have it," Karina said, seeing Dustin move toward the backpack.

He looked over at her in protest, but realized it was no use; he knew the kids needed it more than him. He tried asking the other group what was going on in Europe. There was a father, three kids, and a mother; at least that's what Dustin surmised.

"Where is this train going?" Dustin asked politely.

"Athens, Greece," The father of the group said curtly. "This train stops a lot though, it will be a while before we get there."

. . .

"I have a possible solution for your . . . ah . . . house guest," Dr. Miller said to Jeremy over the phone. "I'm not sure if you know this, Jeremy, but I used to work for the Navy. I helped in the telemetry of some of our guided missiles, and well, there's an old friend of mine from those days who might be able to help you. He lives near Houston. His name is Major Anton Winter. I told him you were coming. He is currently living in a mansion with a group of former Marines; he has been ever since this whole comet business got started. Anyway, I'm sure he'd be able to help you, and you can trust him."

Dr. Miller gave Jeremy Major Winter's address and hung up, telling him he needed to get back to work. Jeremy looked back over to Anna and asked if she'd be up for an adventure.

"Yes!" Anna replied.

Jeremy drove the mom van one hour north toward

Major Winter's mansion. It was in the middle of a sparse forest, which was actually near where Jeremy and his friends had camped just after they'd found out about the comet. Jeremy looked at the mansion in amazement. It had two winding white staircases leading up to an elevated front terrace. There were tall white Corinthian columns encircling the house, which held up a second terrace. Hanging down from the second level was a large yellow flag with a snake on it, which Jeremy recognized as the Gadsden flag.

"Don't Tread on Me," Jeremy read.

They walked up the stairs to the front, where a large man with a gun stood, surveying the grassy parking lot in front of him.

"Hi, um, we're here to see Major Winter," Jeremy asked the guard.

Predictably, the guard didn't so much as look at Jeremy, not even moving a muscle.

"Should we just walk in?" Anna asked. The guard reminded her of one of those British guards with the tall furry black hats at Buckingham Palace.

Jeremy got out his wallet and his work pass, which said he worked at the Johnson Space Center. The guard looked over the work ID and photo, and surveyed Jeremy's face. Then he stepped aside.

"Wow," Jeremy muttered once they walked into the main entrance hall. "I had no idea working at the Johnson Space Center would get me into a Marine's military commune."

There were Marines everywhere talking. It was very odd, seeing all these Marines in modern military attire hanging around the antique antebellum architecture and décor. The word *Restaurant* was spray-painted over the room on the right of the hall.

"Excuse me?" Anna asked one of the Marines lounging on the spiral staircase. "Do you know where Major Winter is?"

The Marine pointed over to the restaurant, saying nothing.

So they went to the restaurant and walked through the hanging curtain. They walked into a small foyer where what seemed to be another former Marine stood chewing gum behind a counter.

"Weapons," the hairy man said grossly. He had all sorts of muck in his teeth.

Jeremy handed the man the gun in his waistband, ignoring the look of surprise he knew Anna was giving him. The man checked it, and nodded toward the next curtain. Jeremy walked through the next curtain and saw fifteen tables, all neatly covered with a red tablecloth, with small candelabras and wine glasses, china, and silverware.

"Wow . . . " Anna said, grabbing Jeremy's hand.

There were not many people there for what Jeremy guessed was lunch: a couple sat in the far corner, a group of four sat drinking in the other corner, and a large man with clean military gear sat listening to a radio.

Jeremy and Anna didn't know what to do, but in a minute the military man stood up, and walked over to them. He wore several patches of military significance on his arm, but Jeremy didn't recognize them.

"Hello," the man said.

"Um yeah, hi, are you Major Winter?" Jeremy asked.

"Please, eat something."

Jeremy and Anna looked at each other before the man ushered them to an empty table covered in a scarlet tablecloth. The man walked back toward his table and sat down.

"This is a lot weirder than I thought it was going to be," Anna whispered.

A man wearing a bowtie and a suit came over to fill their water and wine glasses.

"No wine for us, thanks," Anna told the waiter.

The waiter nodded and bowed, taking the glasses back to the kitchen.

"What is this place?" Anna asked after the waiter left.

"I have no idea," Jeremy whispered, "but let's eat and wait for Major Winter to talk to us."

Seeing this military commune made Jeremy think about the state of the world. It was unsafe to go out at night, Soldiers of God were terrorizing citizens in the streets, and at least one fragment of the comet would hit Earth. The stress of the world ending was not something everyone could handle. But now, more than any time in history, stability was paramount to survival. People needed hope.

Their food came. The snazzy waiter put down a big roasted chicken breast in front of Jeremy. As a side there were roasted vegetables, and a baked potato. Jeremy marveled at the exquisite cuisine.

"Enjoy," the waiter said, bowing.

"Thank you," the couple replied, smiling.

They ate voraciously, and spoke little during the entire meal. After he finished eating, Jeremy used the soft cloth napkin to wipe his lips, and smiled at Anna, who still had a mouthful of food. She smiled back with a mouthful of potato and chicken. It was the best meal he'd ever eaten.

"So, you enjoyed your food, huh?" Major Winter said when he noticed they were finished.

"Yes, thank you so much!" Anna remarked, to which Jeremy nodded his head in agreement.

Major Winter pulled up a chair and sat on it backward—so he could rest his enormous forearms on the back of the chair.

"So," Major Winter began, taking a sip of his wine, "you're in a bit of a tough spot. Dr. Miller told me about your predicament."

Jeremy and Anna looked at each other.

"Yeah," Jeremy responded, "Dr. Miller said we could go to you for help. The man is at our house in Houston now."

Now that Jeremy wasn't starving, he took a better look at Major Winter. Major Winter wore a thick, curly beard, and had a characteristic military-style buzz cut. He was very dark-skinned. He wore glasses, which served to reduce the amount of stereotypes you could place this man in. He had a very kind smile, but a hard face, sharp and angled and square. He had on the same tactical military-grade attire that they had seen all around this mansion. He also didn't have a gun in his holster, and Jeremy asked him why.

"Oh! Not in the restaurant. No restaurant shooting in my joint. I check mine like everyone else before coming in. In an apocalyptic world like the one we are living in, you have to be armed; I'm just thankful that it doesn't have to be one hundred percent of the time."

"That makes sense," Jeremy responded. "And about our situation?"

Major Winter took another sip of wine.

"Bring him here. We can take care of it."

"Really? That would be so great, Major, thank you."

"Don't mention it," Major Winter answered. "If there is anything you need, I am on your side." The Major spoke in a soft voice. "We all want to live, and the right side of the battle is on the side of the United States of America. Any friend of Robert Miller's is a friend of mine. Whatever I can do to help."

"Thank you, Major. I really appreciate it."

"Anytime," the Major said, patting Jeremy on the back and walking slowly back into the kitchen.

The bow-tied waiter came back to clear their plates, and thanked them. Jeremy tried to give the man some ration cards, but he was rebuked.

"No money or bartering here, sir."

They walked back out to the foyer of the room, the security guard gave Jeremy back his gun, and they walked back to their car, feeling thoroughly refreshed and relaxed.

The next day, Jeremy went to the JSC to work, even though he didn't have much to do anymore. Mr. Wilkinson hadn't been to the office since Ian had left, so Jeremy decided to fish for the latest rumor. Some of Jeremy's coworkers said that he was sick. Others said he was sick of wasting time working for the JSC, and had gone to live in Colorado until everything ended. Jeremy wondered if he'd gone to Colorado to find the billionaires' Ark.

10

DOOMED EARTH

July 1, 2017
St. Thomas, U.S. Virgin Islands

It was a cool dark night, or cool for St. Thomas. Robert was hard at work when he should have been sleeping and the seventy-three degree night was not helping him. His shirt was drenched in sweat and his thighs stuck to the chair because he was only wearing boxer briefs.

Finally though, by two in the morning, he had finished the completed model for the comet's trajectory and their bombing strategy. The comet would fragment in one week's time. He printed out the sheets he needed and emailed the rest to President Chaplin and Secretary Brighton. He ran down to the hotel elevator—and then ran back because he remembered he wasn't wearing any pants. He threw some on, and ran back out, down the elevator, right out into the hallway and knocked harshly on room 1004.

"Nick! Brighton! I need to speak to you."

Brighton was up as well, drinking a Scotch in the dark and thinking about his wife. He got up and answered the door.

"What is it, Robert?"

"I've got it, and I wanted to tell you so you could tell the public. If this works, we are going to have our work cut out for us."

"Do you ever think, Robert," the Secretary began, slowly stirring the drink in his hand with his index finger, "that we should have given up when we realized the comet was coming? Lived out our last two and a half years happily, instead of working a hundred hours a week to try to stop something that is so big it will vaporize all of us? Did that ever enter your mind? Or do you just not look at things that way? I mean,

I could have just lived out the last moments happily with my wife in Georgia until we all died."

Robert calmed down from his excitement, and put an arm around his friend, saying, "Listen, Nick. Of course I've thought about that. Who hasn't? Anyone who works that long on something worries that it might not happen how they want. But listen. Don't only think of your own wife. Think of all of the other wives, husbands, sons, daughters, and people we love. Think of the mothers and fathers. Think of my own daughter, and granddaughter. We are the old guys—we could stand to live another few years in peace, but what about the young ones—the people that haven't had a chance to live full lives? We have to save the world for them, not for us."

Secretary Brighton looked down at his glass, then look back up at Robert, and with tears in his eyes, said, "You know, I never thought something you would say would make me cry, but I guess there's a first time for everything." He sighed and took a drink, as if to compose himself. "Okay, what do you got?"

"Well. I've changed a few of the next IMPs to force a break that will be easier for us to handle. The three resulting comets will have three different sizes. 'Comet One' is scheduled to hit in eleven months' time. According to the model I've created, it should land somewhere inside the 47th latitude and the third longitude."

"Jesus Christ. Isn't that France?"

"Very good, Mr. Secretary."

"We'd better call Paris. Where will the others go?"

"The other two comets will hit Earth approximately six months after the impact of 'Comet One.' 'Comet One' will be seven kilometers, 'Comet Two' will be twenty, and 'Comet Three' should be around one and a half kilometers. This is the most crucial information: we must stop 'Comet Two' from hitting Earth—it is now the only comet that would classify as an extinction-level event. I have a trustworthy source at the JSC who tells me that a lot of people aren't showing up to work—like they have given up. We have to fix that problem. And we are going to need more IMPs."

Secretary Brighton nodded. "Comets one and three won't cause widespread damage?"

"They'll cause a lot of damage, but they won't kill everyone like Comet Two. It's my hope that a victorious boost like this fracture could improve morale, and will motivate the people to work again as well. We've successfully given the people at least six more months to live!"

Secretary Brighton shook his head and spoke, "Well, maybe it will give people hope. And we may be able to do something about that second comet. At least now we have more time to figure it out. But first I'm calling Europe, and letting them know that it's their turn to become refugees . . . again."

Robert and Secretary Brighton shook hands, and Robert returned to his room, excited and tired, but not sleepy. He plopped down on his bed, thinking about Jennifer, hoping his daughter was okay.

· · ·

Jeremy got to Major Winter's mansion early. He left his only gun with Anna, and brought some sugar and salt, thinking he might be able to trade the goods for another firearm. He walked in and noticed significantly fewer people than before, and checked his knife at the foyer to the restaurant. He noticed Major Winter eating lunch, and walked over to him. He was eating at the table closest to the kitchen, and had a big bacon cheeseburger in front of him. Seeing it made Jeremy's mouth water.

"Good afternoon, Major. May I sit down?"

"Jeremy, of course. How are you?"

"I brought the prisoner with me," Jeremy replied, taking a seat.

"Okay, just let me finish eating."

Major Winter finished the rest of his burger with one enormous bite and wiped his mouth with his napkin, which was tucked into his shirt. He then took a big swig of his water and leaned back in his chair, picking at his fries.

Jeremy thought about Janice, and went over in his mind what he would say to her when he saw her. He couldn't decide whether he should accuse her of being a spy, or just play it cool. Jeremy looked around. The restaurant looked identical to before. There were groups that he recognized as JSC employees. He nodded at them and they nodded back, and Jeremy wondered how they heard about this unusual restaurant.

Major Winter finished his food, and together they walked out to Jeremy's car, where Ian was tied up in the backseat.

"So this is the terrorist, huh?" Major Winter asked, looking into the backseat. "You've been taking good care of him."

"I guess," Jeremy admitted.

Jeremy had fed him sparingly, but compared to the treatment he had received from Mr. Wilkinson, it was a feast.

Then, Major Winter pulled Ian out of the car, and dragged him by the collar behind the mansion.

"Whoa," Jeremy said. "Wait!"

But Major Winter didn't wait. He flung Ian against the brick wall of the mansion and he collapsed in a heap. Then the Major pulled out his pistol, and aimed it at Ian's temple.

"Wait! Wait!" Jeremy screamed.

Ian closed his eyes and started to murmur, "Go forth, Christian soul, from this world. In the name of God this almighty Father, who created you—"

Major Winter cocked the pistol.

"Shut up!" Jeremy yelled at Ian.

"He's a traitor to the United States. Traitor to the world. He deserves death," Major Winter said grimly.

"Okay, okay," Jeremy said desperately. "But we can't just kill him. He's a traitor, but we can't just execute him."

"*We* aren't," Major Winter said.

"Please," Jeremy pleaded. "Don't kill him. Not yet. Just until I can figure something out."

"You think there's going to be a trial?" Major Winter asked. "There is no court, no judge, no lawyers. All that we have left are executioners."

"Just a few weeks, Major, just a few weeks. I know he's a terrorist, but wouldn't we be the same if we just murdered him? Just a few weeks, Major, please just hold him."

Major Winter kept the gun next to Ian's temple, while Ian continued to mutter verses from the Bible. Finally, Major Winter abated, dropping the gun to his side. Ian let the air out of his lungs and collapsed on the floor.

"One week," Major Winter said, relenting, "But if you don't think of something, he's dead."

• • •

"What can we do?" Anna asked anxiously. "He can't just kill him!"

Anna and Jeremy talked in front of the factory where Anna worked while she was on a break.

"What other choice do we have?" Jeremy responded. "Let him go? Keep him here forever? I don't know what to do, but I have to go back and talk to Major Winter. Maybe I'll figure something out on the way."

Seven days had passed, and he had to go back to Major Winter's mansion—otherwise Major Winter would shoot Ian Hosmer. On top of everything else, Janice the Traitor had called him the day before, and asked to see him, so he told her to meet him outside Major Winter's mansion.

"Just do what your heart tells you," Anna said, referring to both crises. They kissed and Jeremy hopped into his car and sped off to Major Winter's.

He waited, leaning on his car, until Janice rolled up and parked next to him.

"Hey, Jeremy!" Janice said.

"Hey Janice, how have you been?" Jeremy asked, crossing his arms. *Why did you betray me?* Jeremy thought.

"Listen," Janice began, "I'm leaving to go back to Colorado. I'm going on the Ark."

Jeremy raised his eyebrows, waiting for Janice to continue.

"And I want you to come with me—on the billionaires' spaceship. I've been doing a lot of thinking lately and . . . " Janice looked momentarily down at her hands until looking back up at Jeremy. "Would you maybe want to do that? I—I love you, Jeremy."

Janice's eyes flickered back and forth, trying to find an answer from Jeremy's face.

Whoa, Jeremy thought, taken aback. His surprise quickly turned to anger, though, and as Janice leaned closer to him, as if searching for something, he spoke.

"First of all, I have a girlfriend. Second of all, I thought you were trying to help us stop the comet from coming, but now you're just going to run away from the Earth with the richest people in the world? And most importantly, you betrayed me! You lied to me."

"What are you talking about?" Janice asked, sounding hurt.

Jeremy became livid. *How can you still not admit to this?*

"I told you when the plane was going to take off, and you gave that information to the billionaires. You helped kill all those scientists—all those innocent people. It was you! How could you?! HOW COULD YOU DO THAT?!" Jeremy yelled angrily.

Suddenly Janice burst into tears. "I don't know, I don't know! I didn't know that they would kill them. I swear to God. I wanted to go back on the Ark so I agreed to help them get information. I let them put a recording device on me when we were talking, and when I was working in the computer chip factory. I didn't know they were going to use that information to kill people! I had no idea," Janice choked. "I just want to live. Please, Jeremy, you have to believe me."

Janice tried to put a hand on Jeremy's shoulder.

"Get away from me," Jeremy spat, disgusted. "You betrayed us. You may not have meant to harm anyone but you did. I'm not going with you. You're a coward! Go to hell."

Jeremy spun around, angrier than ever, and walked toward Major Winter's mansion. He found him on the second story, looking out of the window. Jeremy presumed he'd notice his argument with Janice.

"Did you make your decision?" Major Winter asked.

Jeremy was still fuming from his confrontation with Janice. *And to think she was in love with me?* Jeremy wondered. He couldn't believe that, but the end of the world made people feel surprising things. Jeremy tried to concentrate on his problem with Ian.

He still didn't know what to do. He had nowhere to put him in prison, and he couldn't bring him back to the government because they would torture him. He didn't want to kill him, but didn't know what else to do.

"He admitted to trying to kill a plane full of people—and succeeded in killing most of them. I think we both know what needs to be done," Jeremy said slowly.

"Very well," Major Winter replied. "You don't have to be here if you don't want, Jeremy."

"No," Jeremy replied. "It's my decision. I should be."

It all happened very quickly after that. Major Winter pulled Ian Hosmer out of the locked room where he was being held. Major Winter brought him to the back of the mansion while Jeremy walked behind them both. Ian mumbled Bible verses to himself.

"Any last words?" Major Winter asked.

Ian Hosmer kept mumbling Bible verses and Jeremy looked away. The barrel of Major Winter's .357 Magnum revolver rotated as the trigger level pushed the hammer backward until it reached a critical point, and then it flung forward and hit the primer, which ignited the gunpowder and drove the bullet down the barrel and into Ian Hosmer. His body slumped to the ground.

11

THE WAITING GAME

July 7, 2017
St. Thomas, U.S. Virgin Islands

"It should happen sometime today," Robert told the assembled team. President Chaplin had flown in from Washington, and there was a live feed of the comet in front of them. For being such a large comet, and for it being the possible catalyst for a real life Armageddon, it always surprised Robert how peaceful it looked. It did not look like it was capable of creating another ice age, gargantuan tsunamis, and the death of life on Earth.

"The comet J312 is now around halfway in between the orbits of Jupiter and Saturn. Within the next few hours we should see the comet split into three separate comets. At this point—according to modeling carried out by Suri Lahdka and myself—one comet, 'Comet One,' will impact Earth on June 10th, 2018, and the other two fragments will collide with Earth in December 2018. Gerald Jan"—Robert motioned over to Gerald standing nearby before continuing—"will launch Project Vishnu tomorrow. This is essentially a spaceship, or space station, which has been modified to orbit the larger of the two fragments, a colossal comet with a diameter of twenty kilometers. It will be a manned mission, and the astronaut who has volunteered for this incredible mission is Dr. Nia Rhodes. She would be here today but she is making preparations for launch. The spaceship Vishnu will orbit 'Comet Two,' with a diameter of twenty kilometers, in an attempt to steer it out of Earth's path."

A brief spell of dismay and despair coated the room, and the air felt thicker.

"Are you saying," President Chaplin began, "that we need to prepare for an impact one year from now?

There is nothing you can do to stop this comet from hitting us?"

"Our primary concern should be Comet Two, because it has the capability of destroying all life on Earth. As destructive as the other fragments will be, the other two fragments do not. With our remaining nuclear weapons, we need to focus on Comet Two."

President Chaplin did not look convinced, but nodded for Robert to continue.

"The Vishnu Space Station will come in handy against those other two comets as well, since it'll be able to orbit them."

"Dear Lord," Mr. Atkins said. "So at this point an impact is completely unavoidable?"

"Yes," Robert responded. "But in a way this is good news. We will also be able to monitor the now three comets very closely and we have bought ourselves some time. The world will not end when the comet splits, and this is due to our great work here. The world will not end on June 10th, 2018."

At first when Robert spoke to the other scientists

on his team, those from Europe were greatly opposed to letting the initial fragment hit Europe. However, as they looked at Robert's model and thought, they slowly realized that there was no alternative. All of the diversion energy had to be used against the largest comet.

There was some nervous applause from around the room when Robert stopped speaking. At this point, it was a waiting game. They watched the screen as the LSST's footage showed the IMPs bombing the comet. They waited nervously. Once they saw how the comet would break, they could determine how accurate Robert's model was. He was very anxious to see how accurate he was; the fate of the world was in his hands.

David Atkins formulated a speech for President Chaplin so she could communicate to the people. It was the government radio channel, so the entire world could hear the president's words. At least, the countries that still transmitted the information would.

Now it was time to play the waiting game. There

was not much more they could do now that the IMPs were *en route* and going to split the comet. Robert knew that it would be devastating if his calculations were incorrect. Right now, the entire population of Western Europe was moving south as quickly as possible. In most circumstances, the waiting was the worst part of any event. Waiting for the job to email you, or waiting to be accepted into college, or even going to war. The waiting game always takes a heavy toll on mental health, and now, the entire world waited.

• • •

"What should we do?" Karina asked Dustin, terrified. The man sitting across from them, a carpenter from Germany, had just told them the news that the comet would hit off the coast of France.

"Let's just try to get as south as possible."

"South where?" Karina asked. "Africa?"

"No. That seems risky. Maybe we could go to

Israel, with a little luck our U.S. passports will still work there."

"You think we could get on a boat?" Karina asked.

"That's what we're going to do," the man who had shared the news told them.

The train was heading to Athens. They were going to get off somewhere in northern Italy to head to Rome, but it seemed they needed a plan that would take them farther south.

"We'll try to find a ship traveling to Tel Aviv or maybe to Haifa. Then, we can go south from there."

It seemed that it would be Europe's turn to become refugees, and head into the nations they had closed their borders to. Dustin and Karina had no choice but to go south as well.

As they barreled down the tracks in Macedonia, they ate nuts that Dustin carried in his backpack, and they went to the bathroom in between the train cars.

By the time the train was almost to Athens, Dustin and Karina didn't know how they were going to pay for the ferry. They had spent most of their time sleeping on the train, and as a result were well rested when it arrived. The train station in Athens was a complete mess. It was swimming with people, all of whom were trying to get out of Europe. They looked around and saw a sea of people, all mostly European, rushing down to the subway to get to Piraeus, the port of Athens. Karina and Dustin jammed their way in, wearing their backpacks on their chests.

The military stood everywhere, trying to keep order, but it was complete mayhem. There were people everywhere, arguing and trying to get onto the boats. The passenger freighters were enormous and everyone was packed into every nook and cranny possible. Dustin and Karina managed to push their way onto a large cruise liner, which was definitely over capacity. Dustin hoped the boat would make it across the Mediterranean without sinking.

They didn't know where exactly they were going. Dustin was surprised by the amount of chaos at the port, especially since there were still eleven months until impact. Both of them kept their backpacks to their front side, so people wouldn't steal their supplies. Dustin felt nervous as more and more people crammed themselves onto the boat, running up the ramp into it. The last thing he wanted was to drown. He'd always read that was the worst way to go, and since he now found himself dealing with death almost daily, the way he would die suddenly became important to him.

Finally, the boat started its engine and began to depart, while people were still running up the ramp, trying to get on.

Dustin and Karina did not see the families they rode the train with again, but found new families and people, escaping the European mainland to ensure safety. Dustin and Karina found themselves on the second level of the ship, leaning on the side of what would normally be a bar. An older Greek gentleman stood next to them, and must have noticed how they stood out since he began to speak.

"You are not European," he began, "Where are you two from?"

"We are from the United States."

"Ah, and you are stuck in Europe and fleeing now with all of us, yes?" The man had twinkling eyes and his accent was mild for such an old Greek. Dustin had read somewhere that most Greeks from the older generation did not speak English.

"That's right," Karina answered.

"Yes, it is funny. When I was just a boy, so many Europeans tried to escape to Africa and the Middle East, running away from Hitler and the Nazis. And now, all of Europe tried to push the Syrians and the Arabs away, for the past twenty years! Now, we are all trying to go there! The world is an ironic place, is it not?"

The man laughed a slightly wheezing laugh, the kind of laugh from a lifelong smoker. Jeremy and Karina exchanged a glance, then returned to looking outside at the ocean, swirling all around them.

"Where is this boat going?" Karina asked.

"Smyrna. You probably call it Izmir, the Turkish coastal city."

Dustin had never heard of the city. *Hopefully they have a working U.S. Embassy*, he thought.

The weather was not good, but they were on their way out of Europe, and after all they had been through to get there, it seemed ironic they would now be fleeing it smashed cheek to cheek in a cruise liner heading for Turkey.

• • •

Janice Effran watched solemnly as her bag was brought into the hull of the Ark. Her father Charlie nodded at her while straightening his tie. She looked away, racked with guilt. When she had left the Ark Project, she really wanted to be done with it. It was disgusting that the billionaire friends of her father—as well as himself—were trying to recreate a new world. It reminded Janice of apocalypse movies, or James Bond villains. They always thought what they were doing was right, and in the end it all came down to selfishness. *What was I thinking, telling Jeremy I loved him? I must have been out of my mind,* she thought. *Why did I betray my country?*

When Jeremy said he was going back to help Dr. Miller stop the comet, she had actually started working for the government as well. She had sincerely believed they could do it. Then, she saw what happened in Miami, and how so many of the people she worked with were making mistakes, and the Soldiers of God were becoming a larger presence and taking control of parts of the country. She called her father, asking for her seat back on the Billionaire's Ark. He said yes, but with strings attached: she would have to feed him information on the government's activity in Houston.

Only after the bombing of the plane did she realize, with shattering horror, that it was her leaks that caused the terrorist attack. The billionaires were using the Soldiers of God to destroy the Earth so they could repopulate it their way. She had no idea her leaked information would lead to death.

She learned a week after the plane bombing that

her father had secured her a seat on the Ark once again. She was beside herself with guilt over what had happened. She was about to refuse the spot he had just reacquired, before she came to a realization: She would have to play the long game. She made a mistake by spying for the wrong people, and now she would make up for it. For now, that meant sitting tight and waiting. She hated her father, and what the billionaires stood for. And she'd asked Jeremy to come for . . . well, she didn't know why. She cared for him, yes, but it wasn't that kind of love. Or was it? Maybe she just wanted a friend on the Ark. Someone she could trust. Anyways, telling him that had been a mistake. She hadn't been in her right mind. In all likelihood he wouldn't have been allowed onboard anyways, but her guilt had caused her to think irrationally. Now, though, waiting to board, she realized that she could spy on the Ark. She would be a mole. She just had to figure out how to communicate with the government from their orbit.

Around four hundred people would go onto the

Ark. There were seeds, nutrient-rich soil, and even some domesticated animals. In addition to the billionaires who had used their influence and money to buy their way, there were also those on board with exceptional skills. There was Xavier Daniels, renowned astronaut and ex-Air Force pilot, who was to captain the Ark. He was accompanied by many other ex-military personnel who would also go aboard to help with day-to-day operations while in the air.

There were drug tests every week for those who were getting on the Ark, as well as health examinations. The main leader was a man named Raymond Kaser. Some of the world's smartest engineers and scientists were on board. There were some young boys and girls who had "perfect genetics," according to one of the scientists. The Four Hundred Prophets, as some of them arrogantly thought of themselves, were incredibly diverse. There were two hundred men and two hundred women. Unsurprisingly, the Pope had stayed with the people, declining his invitation.

They would be in orbit as long as Mr. Kaser

deemed necessary, but the Ark only had enough food for five years, including the food they brought and the food they planned on growing in the Earth-like eco-system portion of the Ark.

Janice sat in her seat in the launch vessel of the Ark, ready for liftoff. On her right was her father, but on her left was someone who had been "stolen" from NASA. He was some kind of engineer, but Janice couldn't remember what.

"I'm a rock expert," the man had said, attempting to flirt with Janice. "I just love rocks."

"That's so interesting," Janice said vaguely.

"Comet J312 could hold vast amounts of Iridium, Rhodium, and Rhenium. Once we touch back down on Earth, it will be my job to extract what we can from the crash sites. I just hope the crash sites are on land . . . The sites should provide some interest-ing clues as to the composition of what's below the Earth's surface! It's such an exciting time to be a sci-entist. Some engineers are working on forcing one of the comet's fragments to orbit Earth. We could have a near-infinite supply of . . . "

Janice couldn't listen to the man anymore, thinking she would kill him if he kept talking.

"Don't you even care that the entire world is going to die?" she interrupted.

The man was taken aback by her abrupt and abrasive question, and replied, "Well, I mean, there was a good chance the world was going to die anyway. At least now we can have control over it."

Janice tuned the man out, but he did not stop talking about his scientific aspirations. Janice simply bided her time, and for the first time in her life, she prayed. *Please, forgive me for what I've done. Please. I will be a good person, and I will make the right and good choice in the future. I am sorry, please forgive me.*

12

THE THREE-HEADED MONSTER

Saturday, July 8, 2017
Somewhere near Shiva's surface

It was the fourth IMP that did it on July 8th, 2017. The specific IMP, Interplanetary Missile Forty-Seven, had quite the multicultural background. Its plutonium had been enriched in Leningrad, and then exported to New Orleans. The computer that governed its flight path was assembled in Houston, so the computer was local at least. The semiconductors were made in China. The hull was from South Africa, and then sent on a commercial freighter to the Port of Houston.

It traveled toward the comet, and at five hundred miles from its surface it turned on its reverse thrusters to slow its speed. The IMP had to hit the comet at just the right time in its rotation for it to reach its weakest point. There was some luck involved, and a lot of hours spent coding, modeling, building, and calculating. The IMP's nuts and bolts were rattling and its fuel was almost used up. Then, finally, the IMP exploded—a terrific eruption of energy discharged radially from the nuclear weapon—and a soundless attack of heat and radiation shot toward the comet. The comet then yielded to the nuke's awful power, beginning to fragment. Far behind the comet, a video satellite sent footage back to the small island of St. Thomas in the Caribbean.

The IMP exploded and the energy from the nuclear blast tried, as it always did, to find the path of least resistance. In this case, the structural integrity of the comet finally gave way, and rapidly split through the middle. The split of the comet created a completely new orbit for the resulting fragments. The blast broke apart the great mass of ice, rock, and dust, and unfortunately the explosion occurred during the daytime. This meant that Robert couldn't see the explosion in the sky, since the Sun's light masked its light burst. However, those on the other side of the world would have seen a small flash of light in the sky, near Jupiter.

· · ·

Robert looked nervously at the screen watching photos sent every 106 seconds. The comet was still more than a billion kilometers away, and since the photos traveled at the speed of light, he had a delay of about seventy-four minutes before he could see how accurately his model showed the comet's fissure and resultant velocity vectors.

The data came in and the team of scientists got to work immediately on analyzing it. Dr. Campero, Dr. Ivanov, Robert, and the rest of the team jumped in while President Chaplin and Secretary Brighton held their breath.

Robert discovered that he was astoundingly close in his model—Suri's model. It happened. The main comet had split into three!

"Three parts like the head of Cerberus," Secretary Brighton murmured.

"What?" Robert asked, distracted.

"He guards the Gates of the Underworld in Greek mythology. Like Cerberus, it seems this three-headed monster will judge the fate of Earth."

Robert didn't answer, still looking over his work. He was correct that Comet One would in fact land somewhere on the western edge of the Eurasian Plate, albeit a little more south than Robert had expected. All the scientists and engineers looked at their screens as the data populated. A scientist that Secretary Brighton previously had no contact with, a Dr. Boris Klaskov, sat in the room as well, patiently listening to everyone else.

"I'm getting France," Robert called out.

"Yes, me too," said Dr. Ivanov.

"I've got Comet One measuring around six kilometers," Dr. Campero said.

"Just as we predicted," Robert said, elated.

"No, but still a killer." Dr. Ivanov paused. "Eet vill likely mean destruction for most of Europe."

"When?" asked President Chaplin.

The sound of keys rapping into keyboards filled the room.

"June second, 2018."

"We've got to alert them. They've got to go underground."

"We've all got to go underground."

"What about the other fragments?" asked Secretary Brighton.

"We need more data before we can know for sure. For now we can accurately say that they'll hit sometimes in December 2018. But, Madam President, Secretary Brighton, Mr. Atkins, the world will not end in June 2018. We will survive."

This was cause for excitement, as the world would survive the initial fragment hit. The comet would be devastating for life, and likely all of Europe would be destroyed. In fact, the entire world would have to go underground for days, possibly weeks or months. As for Robert and the rest of his team, they had to go back to Los Alamos with the president. They would have to go deep underground, since the impact from the comet would drastically increase the temperature so much that any humans outside after the impact would be cooked alive.

"Okay," Robert said, after reading enough information. "The fragment will hit off the coast of France, destroying much of Europe. Completely incinerated. I will turn over now to Dr. Boris Klaskov. He is the head of Team Apocalypse, or the team responsible for our post-comet protocol. I assume we will be going soon underground?"

"That is correct. For those of you who don't know me," the Ukrainian said, in a slightly British accent, "my name is Boris Klaskov, I am originally from Kiev. My team and I have been working since the comet was discovered to develop plans and infrastructure for post-impact survival. I have been retrofitting the bomb shelters of the United States—my adopted home country—and teaching all other nations how to build their own bomb shelters.

"For the United States, we are far enough away from the impact itself that we will only receive the secondary effects. The devastation, hours after impact, will be global. We must go underground as quickly as possible. We will take shelter at the Los Alamos National Laboratory, which has a sufficient underground bunker. Since the comet will land very near the coast of France—and consequently in shallow ocean—much of the debris from the impact will be ejected into the atmosphere. There will also be a large mega-tsunami that will affect much of the eastern United States, as well as this island.

"When the ejecta falls back down to Earth, it will increase the global atmospheric temperature by thousands of degrees. This is why we need to be underground. Anything that is not will be incinerated. Meanwhile humans will have to rely on MREs

(Meals Ready to Eat) which we've been manufacturing at a high rate since the discovery of the comet. The comet may have an effect on our electronics, so much of our work in farming and manufacturing after the comet might need to be done through human-operated tools. Communication might be altered as well—with a comet impact like this we can form many hypotheses, and model many outcomes, but truthfully we have little evidence or experience in large impacts to Earth. We are doing everything to prepare, and during the next year we will continue to create as much infrastructure as we can to make sure as many people survive the impact as possible.

"Now, the location of the impact is also problematic," Dr. Klaskov said, continuing full-speed. "Since it is in the ocean there will be a tsunami starting from the point of impact. However, in the event the comet actually penetrates the Earth's crust, lava and sulfur will be ejected, which could be locally catastrophic. The impact might awaken long-dormant volcanoes, such as Kilimanjaro, or Ararat. The impact may also dramatically increase the amount of seismic activity in the world. Broken gas lines will cause massive fires. And with the temperature soaring, the vegetation will be tinder dry and ignite, causing a massive conflagration. Also, it is possible an electromagnetic pulse will affect infrastructures related to energy, communications, and any other electronically controlled objects or systems."

After hearing this, the room fell silent.

"I know this is a lot, but at this point any or none of these events will occur. All we can do is model and predict. My colleague, Dr. Samuel Olidi, is an expert in botany and post-apocalyptic farming methods. He and I are building a network of underground farming facilities around Los Alamos, complete with UV lights, irrigation, and much more."

"Thank you, doctor," Robert replied, remembering to insert another useful piece of information. "We must also thank Gerald Jan, whose Vishnu spaceship successfully launched and is now on its way to Comet Two, which is twenty kilometers in size. We expect it to begin orbiting Comet Two soon. We will continue IMP production and launch toward Comet Two, resetting coordinates to attempt to move it. A long hibernation will begin soon after impact, gentlemen, and we need to tell the people of the world to go underground or perish. This is one of the greatest genetic bottlenecks the world has ever seen, and we must try our hardest to come through the other side."

• • •

"What should we do?" Anna asked, nervously.

"I called Robert," Jeremy replied. "He told me that people are going to have to go underground, but the impact is still eleven months off. He said something about West Virginia, but I want to talk to Major Winter, too. Maybe he has an idea."

"West Virginia? Why West Virginia?"

"There's a river there, it's subterranean. It goes

underground, and when the comet hits, there's a large possibility that it will cause a lot of small rock particles to eject into the atmosphere. Then, when they fall back down, they'll basically be little fireballs, and the temperature of the Earth will be so high that it will kill anything that's above ground. So, we'll have to be underground. He couldn't tell us where he was going to be, not that it matters. He can't take us with him."

"Wow, I can't believe it's really happening. The end of the world—I never thought—even when the comet was coming, I never thought it would actually hit."

"Call your parents and tell them to go underground. There are a lot of places that the government has been building that will house people. But, it's first come, first serve. Tell them to find a bunker. If they can't, tell them to build one. At the very least they *have* to go underground."

"What about your parents?"

"I don't know," Jeremy admitted. He hadn't

talked to them in a month, after he'd argued with them. And then Ian Hosmer became his prisoner, which had taken up most of his time. Even though he'd been angry at them, he wanted to make sure his parents were okay.

• • •

Suri woke up from a long sleep feeling much clearer than she'd felt in months. Her physical therapy had been going well, but her psychiatric help had been moving along less smoothly. Today, though, she felt noticeably better; more *alive*, somehow. As she was being moved from her hospital in St. Thomas onto a plane, she noticed the air was sweet and dewy in the morning.

As she was pushed in a wheelchair toward Air Force One, which would take her back to Los Alamos, she saw Robert walking up ahead.

"Robert," she called.

He waited for her.

"I think I'm ready to start working again."

Robert raised his eyebrows, excited.

"Just in time," he said. "We've got our work cut out for us."